A Fair Collection

Tabbie Browne

Copyright © 2014 Tabbie Browne

All rights reserved, including the right to reproduce this book, or portions thereof in any form. No part of this text may be reproduced, transmitted, downloaded, decompiled, reverse engineered, or stored, in any form or introduced into any information storage and retrieval system, in any form or by any means, whether electronic or mechanical without the express written permission of the author.

This is a work of fiction. Names and characters are the product of the author's imagination and any resemblance to actual persons, living or dead, is entirely coincidental.

ISBN: 978-1-326-06881-3

PublishNation, London
www.publishnation.co.uk

Other titles by this author

White Noise is Heavenly Blue (Book One of The Jenny Trilogy)
The Spiral (Book Two of The Jenny Trilogy)
Choler (Book Three of The Jenny Trilogy)
The Unforgivable Error
No – Don't!

Visit the author's website at:
www.tabbiebrowneauthor.com

Chapter 1

"The alarm will go off in a minute and spoil this lovely moment," thought Jan as she studied the naked sleeping form of her husband lying on his belly at her side. "My God, you're handsome" she murmured.

Steve Masters was indeed handsome, he stood an erect 5' 10", was well built, without any surplus fat, and his blond wavy hair and deep set blue eyes had made many a heart flutter during his thirty five years. He was one of those people that seemed to improve with age, and one could imagine him being a stunner in his sixties.

Janet Masters was three years younger, carried a trim figure, and wore her dark brown hair cut in a simple style, fairly short. She always looked immaculate. They made a fine couple, both very much in love after their eleven years of marriage.

A slight movement from Steve encouraged Jan to slip her arm across his back until her lips brushed his ear.

"C'mon sleepy, we're at Rugby today." A heavy lidded eye reluctantly opened.

"Mmm, I'd rather stay here with you angel," breathed Steve as he manoeuvred himself until he had Jan firmly in his arms.

"So would I, but we have to go, we've booked our table." At which point Jan was backed up by the alarm which shattered the early morning peace as if on cue.

"O.K. angel, be a love and make some tea while I have a shower."

Jan slipped on a gown, trotted downstairs and busied herself making breakfast and a packed lunch. These stamp fairs could be tiring and there wasn't always a chance to buy food, besides which it was cheaper to take your own. When she had finished, Steve appeared.

"Bathroom's free. I'll load the car while you're getting ready." and he gave his wife a loving pat on the bottom as she passed.

Stamp fairs had become a popular trend in the philatelic world in the seventies. They were held in hotels or public rooms in cities nationwide, which gave people a good chance to buy from or sell to several dealers, if the collectors weren't lucky enough to have a local shop. The dealers were either professional or "part-timers" dealing mainly at week ends. Occasionally, tours would be arranged travelling for about a week in one area, doing a fair per day.

The local fair organisers were a firm trading as "We Are Stamps" with three local shops. Two of the managers decided to run the fairs, but also have a stand at each event.

Brian Dakin had been with the firm for fifteen years, was rather a quiet stable sort of chap, could almost be described as uninteresting, but he knew his stuff which was important. He had been made manager of the High Street shop when it opened eight years before, and was lucky enough to have a good salesman, that he could safely leave in charge when he was away.

Brian was somewhere in his fifties and had moved into the professional stamp world when he had been made redundant from his engineering job, but he had collected since he was six, and had always studied the subject. His pet love was postal history, and had given many talks to the local Philatelic Society.

His colleague was a live wire and just the opposite. Tony Jennings' shock of red hair matched his nature. Here was a young man of twenty four, who was really going places. He did nothing slowly. A job that would have taken Brian all day, Tony would have finished in a couple of hours. But it would have to be right. He demanded perfection from himself and expected it from others. He was very qualified and could have had any job he wanted, but his love was in stamps, and he was determined to make his money at it. And he would. That was for sure.

By 8.30 am Brian and Tony had the room organised ready for the first arrivals, and while Brian was wandering around re-checking the names on the tables, Tony was setting up their own stand.

"Good morning boys, are we first again?" The voice came from the doorway, which framed the ample shape of Nora Dennis.

"Yes, you're over there Nora, Brian will show you," called Tony, intent on clamping a display to the table.

"Come on Bert" beckoned Nora, "bring the cases over here."

"Yes dear" mumbled her long suffering other half.

"Poor old Bert, not a bad chap," thought Brian "if he wasn't under her thumb so much, and her being such a prude. Bet the poor devil doesn't have much fun. Can't imagine them at it."

Other dealers started arriving, and by nine o'clock most were at their tables, busily setting out their books and displays, with the odd friendly banter being exchanged. There was a noticeable gap next to Jan and Steve until about 9.30, when, in a flurry of agitation, a slim young man planted his case, and himself in the only space remaining. This was Giles Foreman. With his air of "Oh God, aren't you women lucky to have me," he made varied excuses for his late arrival which one couldn't help feeling were all very pre-prepared.

"Giles bragging again?" whispered Steve as Jan tucked the empty cases under the stall.

"He must be" she answered "or he hasn't scored lately and is feeling the strain."

"Some poor female's in for it then" grinned Steve.

Jan shrugged. "I don't reckon he'd be that good."

Giles certainly reckoned he was good. Very good. At twenty eight and unmarried, the world was at his feet. He was a right little "mummy's boy", came from a rather well to do family and had always had life too easy without much effort on his part. No. Giles put his effort in trying to lay every available female in which ever town he found himself. As he did not seem to be able to hold down any regular employment, Mummy and Daddy had set their dear boy up in his own stamp business. There wasn't the remotest chance of it ever being a success, as his interests were always elsewhere. It was a known fact that he would 'pick up a bit' at each fair, and if he had not succeeded by noon, he was, as Jan put it, walking round with it in his hand.

Tony's voice called above the chatter, "Action stations, we're open" and another stamp fair was in full swing.

Chapter 2

"Bert, this young man wants some traffic light gutter pairs. Can you see to him? I must sit down." And Nora Dennis plonked her weight on the only empty chair. There wasn't much room behind a stall, with the empty boxes and reference books, but what space there was, Nora filled it. She fiddled in her overloaded shopping bag, and took out a flask of coffee. Pouring out two small cups, she squeezed one on to the table behind one of the stands, and sipped the other as she viewed the various potential customers.

So this was retirement. Not for them the idle life. They had their hobby, which had turned into a little business, and plenty of time to spend on it. Anyway, she didn't want Bert stagnating in his armchair, puffing away on that pipe. That wasn't good for any man, and certainly not hers.

"Is this mine? Bert having a lull between customers grabbed the coffee eagerly.

"I see the part timers are here." Nora cast her gaze to Jan and Steve Masters.

"Now then love---------"

"Now then nothing." snapped Nora. "He has a job. A schoolteacher isn't he? And she does part time office work, calls herself a temp or something. Why don't they stick to that and leave the trade to those of us that rely on it."

"You can't talk Nora, there's some that says we old 'uns should get out you know."

"Rubbish." said Nora. "Serve that man, he's waiting."

"Can I help you?" enquired Bert, as Nora struggled to her feet, feeling a little refreshed.

"Hey, come back you thieving bitch. The cry silenced the general hum.

"What's up Terry?" called Brian Dakin.

"I've had my eye on that bitch for the last five minutes, and then just when I was serving she nicked one of my C.B.S.s." The book being worth just over £1 did not warrant Terry leaving his stall to chase after the woman, who had by this time disappeared.

Brian stood talking as the drone of conversation gradually resumed, the excitement being over. Making full use of an excuse to leave his stall he decided he'd have a wander round.

"I'll find the Gents first, I could do with a pee." he thought, and set off in the general direction of where he thought they were. At the end of a narrow corridor he found two doors. Ignoring the Ladies he entered the Gents and at first thought he had the place to himself. Standing there relieving himself, he heard a slight noise, and glancing over his shoulder, noticed one of the cubicle doors closing.

"Funny." he mused. "I didn't hear anyone come in." As a rather unpleasant feeling crept over him, he tucked his weapon away, quickly swilled his hands, and set off back to the hall. As he approached his stall he was greeted by Tony calling "Come on Brian, lend a hand, I've got a queue here. Can you sort out the GV1 defins for that gentleman, and have we any Jamaica with us?"

As Brian settled himself to the business of serving, he couldn't help noticing Liz Niebur returning to her stall, giving him a very searching look. A thought crossed his mind.

"It couldn't have been her. Now what made me think that?"

As the fair grew busier, the episode gradually slipped from his mind.

"What's the matter love?" Jan and Steve were having a sandwich as the crowds had dispersed, probably for their own lunch.

"Oh, nothing." Jan still looked worried, so Steve pursued his question. Jan shrugged.

"It sounds silly, but that Liz is looking at me again. She gives me the creeps."

"What, the nympho?" laughed Steve.

"You can think it's funny, and call her what you like" frowned Jan, "but I'm telling you, there isn't a woman here that will go to the loo when she's in there, and I'm always scared in case she follows me in."

"Well, what has she ever actually done?" A smile still twinkled around Steve's lips.

"She's never actually done anything-------"

"Well then," cut in Steve, "what the hell are you worried about?"

"I can't describe it Steve, it's just a very nasty uneasy feeling, that's all."

Liz Niebur gave most people a feeling of some sort. She had dark penetrating eyes that seemed to search out your innermost thoughts. Her black straight, shoulder length hair always looked exactly the same and never seemed to grow. Was it a wig? Among the other traders it was suggested that she never used tweezers to pick up stamps, her nails were long enough! She kept very much to herself, was not one for conversation, yet everyone felt her presence.

Jan cast a glance at Liz, who appeared to be engrossed with a customer.

"Back in a moment," she called to Steve and nipped over to Bert and Nora.

"Nora, do me a favour," whispered Jan, "I'm dying to spend a penny, can you keep Liz in conversation for a minute?" She didn't have to be more explicit. As she had tried to explain to Steve, all the women shared the same view.

"You know I would Jan, if she were there." Jan spun round. No Customer. No Liz.

"Oh God, no. Well I'm just going to have to go Nora."

"Good luck then," Nora said with a wry grin.

Jan found the corridor, gently opened the door marked Ladies and crept in. All seemed empty. With a sigh of relief she dashed to a cubicle, slipped down her frilly briefs and sank gratefully on to the seat. After a moment she heard the door of the next cubicle gently close, and the noise of some-one moving.

"It could be somebody else" thought Jan, "it doesn't have to be her." She gathered her wits as she straightened her clothes.

"Well, here goes", and with a vigorous thrust on the handle, she made as much noise as possible flushing the toilet, as if to boost her spirits.

Opening the door, she hurried to the wash basins. All clear. So far, so good. She was just drying her hands, when she felt a closeness behind her. She spun round to come face to face with the unsmiling Liz. The dark eyes moved over her whole body, stripping, searching, gloating. Jan wanted to run, but found she was riveted to the spot, her hands poised on the towel. She felt a hot serge flow over her body.

"What is she doing to me?" Jan screamed inside, but no sound came from her lips.

Slowly, Liz retreated with a half smile of satisfaction spreading over her mouth. As the door closed behind her, Jan sank into the towel almost sobbing with emotion. But what emotion? Was it fear? Attraction? No, how stupid. How could it be attraction?

The door flew open and in breezed Tricia Bennett, a bright young teenager.

"Hey, what's with you? Have you seen a ghost?"

"No, no, it's O.K. I wasn't feeling too good." Jan began to return to normal, not really knowing what had just happened to her.

"I'll be all right thanks Tricia." She returned to the stand where Steve was busy with some-one wanting to sell a collection. Nora glanced at Jan, then at Liz who seemed engrossed in explaining something very lengthy to some foreign visitors. Jan gradually settled down to the rest of the afternoon, wondering whether or not to tell Steve of the events. But what events? And would he just laugh?

Chapter 3

It was 4pm, and so far Giles had not had any luck in procuring his little bit of talent for the night. Bert Dennis passed his stall.

"What's up Giles? No luck today? Why don't you try old Liz? You'd be all right there."

"I'd rather have it cut off than stick it in that, thanks all the same old boy" said Giles with at grimace.

Bert hurried off and left Giles in a very down, unwanted state. His gaze was fixed at table top level, when he noticed a well clad pair of thighs gracing the edge. As his eyes lifted they rested upon a pair of boobs fit enough to delight any hungry man. And Giles sure was hungry!

The face wasn't too bad either, and it spoke.

"You look a bit down love, has she said no?" The saucy face said "Come and get me" if ever one did. Giles woke up.

"Well now darling, I can't imagine you saying no"

"That depends who's asking." She glanced up at the board. "Giles Foreman. Is that really your name?"

"At your service and pleasure" I hope thought Giles.

Tony Jennings cast a disapproving look towards the little dialogue and clicked his tongue.

"I'm glad he doesn't work for us," he mused, "He wouldn't last five minutes.

After a short exchange of smiles and words, Miss Thighs and Boobs left, giving a little wave in Giles' direction, and just about everyone else knew that was only the beginning. After what Giles considered was a respectable time, at least two minutes, he started to pack up.

Tony appeared in front of the stall.

"You're doing Coventry tomorrow aren't you Giles?"

"Oh yes, if I'm up dear chap."

Reluctantly Tony said "We're doing a tour, south coast, week after next, did you say you were coming?" And silently said a little prayer "Please say no."

"Well of course dear chap, couldn't miss out on that now, could I?"

"More's the pity" groaned Tony under his breath, and aloud "Before you shoot off, how about your stall rent?"

"Give it you tomorrow, must dash."

"Now." insisted Tony.

"Oh, how tiresome. I've hardly taken a penny dear chap."

"Not my fault. Try working harder at it." Tony retorted briskly.

"Oh, I always work hard at it, in fact I will be doing just that very soon", and slapping his money in Tony's hand, he hummed to himself to indicate the conversation was ended.

Tony moved round the room collecting stall rents, and checking on dealers for the south coast tour. It seemed the regular bunch would be there. Jan and Steve could go as it was the end of term, Bert and Nora, Giles unfortunately, Liz Niebur and themselves. Not a bad little convoy.

"It's the usual crowd for the tour Brian," announced Tony as he rejoined his colleague behind the stall "Let us hope it's a good one."

Brian nodded in agreement as he counted the takings.

"Looks as though it was a good one today, have you booked the hotels, by the way?"

"I'm confirming next week, now I know the exact numbers." Tony was only sure it would be correct if he did the job himself.

"Did you see that collection we bought in?" Brian seemed quite excited.

"Mmm" Tony leaned nearer to Brian, "but did you know it had been to every dealer in the room first?"

"No! But then I'm not surprised."

"I've a feeling I've seen it before."

Brian stopped and looked up. "Oh. Where?

Tony shook his head. "I don't know, it just seemed familiar."

Both busied themselves packing up, as most of the customers had gone, and only a few stragglers were left talking to Bert Dennis. Nora was getting restless. If they didn't want to buy anything, why didn't they just go home. She was far too tired to be nice, and Bert would talk until the cows came home. Eventually, they left, and the weary pair were able to head for their little bungalow only an hour's drive away

Chapter 4

"You know what's the best part of doing a fair?" asked Steve as he relaxed after a meal later that evening.

"What's that?" mumbled Jan as she curled up on the settee, her head resting gently upon his lap.

"It's coming home again, and the thought of what I'm going to be doing to you before long." He stroked her hair lovingly.

"You randy man." Jan said jokingly.

"There's nothing wrong with that," her husband retorted, "we're married, I love you, and you like everything I do to you, don't you?"

"Of course I do, and you like what I do to you, like massaging your neck."

"Oh, do it now Jan, it relaxes me so much."

"I daren't, it might get you going."

"Please."

Jan slid round the back of the settee and gently started moving her fingers over Steve's neck. He groaned. She increased the pressure.

"Don't stop, that's wonderful."

As the caressing fingers slipped away, Steve turned to see his wife heading for the door.

"I'm tired" she yawned. "Think I'll have a shower and pop into bed."

"In that case, I'll join you, these fairs always make me feel scruffy." Steve was on his feet in an instant. He quickly switched off the standard lamp and cast a hurried glance over the room to make sure everything was all right.

The sound of splashing water met his ears as he approached the bathroom. Hurrying out of his clothes, he pushed his head into the shower and eyed Jan's delightfully supple body. The sight of her was always enough to raise more than his spirits.

"I'm doing my bit for the economic situation" he joked and stepped under the refreshing fountain.

The Masters had always enjoyed a very uninhibited relationship, one of their mutual pleasures being to caress each other under the shower, with the inevitable result. Each enjoyed a healthy sexual appetite which had been adequately satisfied by the other.

The sudden unexpected reaction startled the grin from Steve's face.

"Oh, you made me jump." Jan's eyes were wide and held a look which could only be described as fear. "I didn't hear you."

"It's O.K. angel." Strong arms enveloped her feminine delicateness as the water trickled over their entwined forms. As she became aware of the intimate contours against her, she was overcome with a horrible feeling of revulsion. A nakedness.

"She has made me feel like this," she thought, the effect of the day's earlier event vivid before her closed eyes.

"I'm tired, let me go." Jan was begging.

Bewilderment spread over the handsome features as Steve looked at the pathetic form he held now at arms length.

"O.K. but I've never seen you like this before, at least not since--" but he let his voice trail away, having no wish to finish the sentence, as Jan pushed past him and grabbed a towel to cover herself, leaving Steve pondering in the shower.

They had no children, although two years after they had married, Jan had given birth to a baby boy. It had been a difficult birth, and the baby had died a few weeks later. After the emotional upset which naturally followed, Jan had picked herself up pretty well. She put on a good outward show, but often felt the pangs whenever she saw a friend's new baby, or a child the age that Stephen jnr would have reached. They had never conceived again, and seemed to throw their whole life into each other.

"Is that what's biting her?" mused Steve as he towelled himself dry, but could not imagine why after so long.

As he padded softly along to their bedroom, he heard muffled sobs, and as he slid into bed he tried to comfort his wife, but she only curled up in a tight little ball, and gently cried herself to sleep.

Steve rolled onto his back and slid his hand to the ache in his groin.

"You had better go to sleep as well boy, you're not wanted tonight."

Chapter 5

"This one has no finesse when it comes to the finer points." The thought flickered through Giles' mind. Miss Thighs and Boobs had Giles well and truly in her grip.

"Gently dear girl" he breathed, "save a bit for some other lucky lady."

"I see your problem," the boobs wobbled in his face. "You haven't got all that much to go round have you? Someone get hungry and bite the end off?" Thinking this remark highly amusing, she burst into a fit of uncontrollable tittering. This did nothing for Giles' ego, or his proportions.

"Look here Sally"

"Sandra" she corrected.

"Yes, - um- Sandra , it isn't the size you know, it's what you do with it that matters."

"I haven't noticed you doing much yet, except yelp every time I grab it," at which point she demonstrated by sinking her nails into his equipment.

"That usually gets 'em going" she remarked most disappointedly, as though she had failed a test.

"Well I prefer something a little more delicate, being a gentleman."

"Ha." she almost swallowed him. "A gent is no different, they're all the same in bed."

"You certainly have been around." Giles was stating a fact rather than asking a question.

"You bet. I've seen 'em all, had some surprises too."

Tonight was not turning out a bit the way Giles had planned. He did not usually have this trouble. A girl was generally more than willing to jump under the covers and let him do the work. That was manly. Yes. But not this. This one was trying to lay him down and do it for him. That would not do for this young man. He had to show a female he was in charge. He must make love to her.

Whilst he was lying there, his face turned away deep in thought, he failed to notice that she had slowly been bringing him back to life.

"I can be gentle, if I've a mind to." She kissed his ear. Then slowly travelled down to his chest, hovered around his waist, before descending further. Giles by this time was really standing to attention. Knowing he could not last long the way things were going, he moved the girl onto her back, despite her protests and finished in a couple of movements what she had hoped could have been much longer lasting. Satisfied, he climbed off and asked abruptly "Where's your bathroom?"

"Through there, but hang about, I've not finished yet."

"But I have," stated Giles as he locked himself in the bathroom.

"You bastard" yelled Sandra "You men only think of yourselves, as long as you've shot your lot you don't give a monkey's toss how a girl feels."

"Charming I'm sure". Giles studied his reflection in the mirror. "Let's be honest Giles, some women just do not know how to appreciate perfection when they see it."

Nora Dennis was wide awake. Bert soundly asleep snored rhythmically across the room. The pair had occupied single beds for some years. They had a married son, which surprised most people, as Nora considered that anything to do with physical contact wasn't quite decent.

Bert had never seen her in the nude, and she had no wish to see him unclad. Her husband was a quiet likeable sort of man, got on with every one and it a waste for him to be stuck with some-one like Nora.

Her mind kept slipping back to Liz Niebur. Now there was a peculiar girl if ever there was. And Jan. She'd been gone a long time. And when did Liz return? That girl came and went like a spirit. There one minute, gone the next. "Shouldn't be surprised if she hadn't got something to do with séances and things." Nora shuddered." Never had much time for that sort of thing, but it makes you wonder." Her mind slipped back to Jan. Not a bad sort but dressed a bit inviting at times. Probably to suit her husband. He was always eyeing her up and down, and giving her friendly caresses. Nora wished they would keep that sort of thing to when they were at home. People didn't want it. Not in public. What if everyone went about mauling people. And that Giles was downright blatant. He would be in trouble before long, or have some girl in trouble anyway. He could do with taking a leaf out of that Tony Jennings book. A nice young man that. Works hard, keeps his mind on his job and doesn't go looking after every bit of skirt that passes him. Make somebody a good husband he will.

So Nora's mind ran on, interrupted by snorts from Bert, in his sleep, safe in his own little dreams.

Liz lived alone. She liked it that way. Her flat, to the outsider would have appeared somewhat foreboding. None of the other stamp dealers had ever seen either the inside or the outside, for no-one really knew exactly where she lived, and that is just how Liz intended it to be. Most of her life was just how she intended it to be. She gave the impression of being totally in charge of every situation, her circumstances and even her fate. She was ruled by nothing, she did the ruling. Not by action or any outward force, one just had the feeling she governed everything from within. She had never been known to lose her temper, but had always made her wishes felt with her calm air, laden with mystery.

The people whose lives brushed hers, had their own ideas. Some thought she was in fact a man, while others were not too sure either way. Men and women alike had felt she had mentally seduced them, an experience no-one was too keen on discussing, not that anyone could have adequately described the feelings experienced.

There were those who were convinced she was a witch, she certainly fitted the description. The occult did not escape attention, and many, like Nora, believed she held regular séances and was in touch with the world beyond. Most people seemed to mix up the whole lot, and looked upon her as something not quite wholesome, and to be avoided at all costs.

It was questioned amongst the dealers as to how Liz managed to sell, without frightening away the customers. Brian had once remarked that she probably cast a spell over them so that they could not leave her stall until they had bought something. This had caused great mirth momentarily, and was re-born in everyone's mind each time a little queue formed round her table.

Liz was not one to socialise, had no actual friends, but in no way could she be described as lonely. The walls of her flat, although decorated in black and dark red wallpaper, were almost covered with the weirdest objects, some collected, and some left to her by relatives. Many items had a distinct Voodoo appearance, and those that would have made most people shudder, gave their owner a feeling of peace. It was not uncommon for her to sit and meditate for hours on end. A large satin cushion was always kept for this purpose, and when not in use, was housed in a special place in the corner, directly under a rather hideous mask.

It was sitting cross legged on her cushion, after having eaten a scanty meal, that Liz spent the evening following the fair. Her mind moved to Jan Masters. The satisfied smile crept over her face.

"Easy. She was so easy. I doubt if her husband will be such a pushover," and her hypnotic eyes fell to mere slits as she concentrated her mind on the next target.

Chapter 6

Tony Jennings had the room set out in the Coventry hotel when Brian appeared. The latter yawned and was about to explain why he hadn't slept too well, when Tony announced

"The boards have to go outside Brian, could you possibly manage that?"

"Eh? Oh yes." It always took the older man several minutes to fall in at this hour. After all it was Sunday, and only 8.30am, he would rather be still in bed.

"Any chance of a coffee?" he enquired on returning after his chore.

"I've ordered some." Tony replied without turning, intent on setting up the stand.

"Can't see this one being brilliant, the weather will put them off. It's pouring again." Brian hovered round the entrance like an expectant father.

"You ordered coffee?" enquired a sweet young thing from an inner door.

"Oh yes can you put it on there please?" Tony gave a nod towards a bare table.

"Seventy five pence please."

Whilst Tony fumbled for the change, Brian helped himself to coffee and sat down.

"I can do with this."

As Tony poured his own coffee he said "Are we taking Martin on tour then?"

Brian thought for a moment. "If they can spare him from the Main Street shop, it would be a good idea. He has done a couple of local fairs, and it is always good to have a standby in case you or I couldn't ever make it."

"We could do with him on the stand, we've got three tables" Tony reminded him " and we can take it in turns on the door, that way he will always have one of us with him."

Brian once again sank into a moment of reverie. "Does he drive?"

Tony nodded. "He's passed his test."

"How old is he?"

"Eighteen."

Brian finished his coffee. "He's a bit on the quiet side, but a likeable enough lad."

"Here's George and the Dragon" breathed Tony as he caught sight of the Dennis's arriving.

Brian looked up. "Hello Nora, Hello Bert" then added "Where are they Tony?"

"Near the door."

"Oh good." Nora rested her bags on the first table, "Got a bit more room today."

"There's not so many standing Nora" called Tony. "All right Bert?"

"Fine thanks" came the barely audible reply as Bert staggered in with the display stands.

Within half an hour, all but Giles Foreman had arrived and were busily setting up. Jan noticed to her horror that they were next to Liz, although Liz seemed to be avoiding Jan's direction. They passed a polite "Good Morning" and both became engrossed in getting ready for the day ahead.

"Thank goodness" thought Jan, "Either she has forgotten, or it was just my imagination yesterday." But she would be on her guard just the same, after all, it wasn't in a crowd when the problems arose.

Had she only known the other girls' intentions, she would not have worked with such an easy mind. Steve was still under the effect of his wife's behaviour and appeared somewhat withdrawn. Jan longed to put her arms round his neck and assure him everything was all right. She would later.

It was five to ten when Giles finally arrived.

"No need to ask which is mine," he announced breezily.

"You've got five minutes, we open at ten," Brian hurried over, and in an undertone enquired "O.K. last night then?" and gave a knowing wink.

"Absolutely splendid dear chap, my word, did I give her what for?" and gave a gesture that made Nora's eyebrows raise at least two inches. Bert couldn't help wondering how Nora knew what it meant in the first place.

"Disgusting." she tutted.

"Oh leave him alone" Bert chastised, and was about to add "I had my moments when I was a young 'un" but took one look at Nora's face, and thought better of it.

Giles hurriedly spread his stock over his stall, and sat back to await the talent parade.

"Let's hope the winds blow something decent in today" he thought as his eyes roved the rather splendid room. "God only knows, I deserve it."

By one o'clock there had been a steady stream of people through the door, but now most seemed to have gone for lunch. A good time for the dealers to grab a bite to eat whilst they had a chance.

Liz appeared to be engrossed in marking up some prices, so Jan seized the chance to slip off to the loo. Her inner fight returning, she sat there thinking "Just try it on today madam , I'm ready for you." The click of a door snapped Jan alert, but she soon recognised the little cough of one of the other girls, so she unhurriedly spent a few minutes freshening up, fiddling with her hair, and checking on her make up. Which was just what Liz anticipated.

As soon as Jan had disappeared, she had asked Steve's advice about a censor mark. As their stalls were alongside, they were almost sitting side by side at the back of one of the displays. Steve turned unawares and caught Liz's gaze, and there she held him for a moment. When she spoke, the words began to fade and he was conscious only of a floating sensation, which gave way to another sensation. He was becoming very much aroused.

As she stopped talking his senses returned. He looked around, but no-one seemed aware of the little occurrence. Her eyes moved down his body until they rested at the top of his jeans.

"God, I'm in a state" he panicked. It was the nearest he had ever been without actually touching it. He wanted to rush to the wash room and cool off but there was no way he could walk across the room as he was. Looking up he saw Jan returning a grabbed a stock book onto his lap to hide the tell tale bulge.

"Did you say you wanted to nip off before we have something to eat Steve?" Jan sat down beside her husband.

"No I -- er, not for the moment." he stumbled over the words. Jan looked worried and did not notice the smile on Liz's face as she watched the little exchange.

"I'm O.K, just a bit tired. Yes I will go. Will you be all right on your own a minute?"

"Sure." nodded Jan.

Steve had almost returned to normal, and headed off towards the door. In the safety of the gents, he dabbed his face with cold water. Staring at his reflection in the mirror he almost said aloud, "What the hell was that?" He felt a mixture of anger at having allowed that woman to have an effect on him, for an effect she certainly had achieved, but the feeling was in a strange way enjoyable. This gave rise to a somewhat guilty reaction as he thought of Jan. She was the only one he wanted to make him feel that way, and yet Liz had succeeded in getting such a strong response, and she knew it. Of that Steve was certain.

What Jan had said the day before and her behaviour in the shower suddenly brought Steve out of his reverie. "She's on her own!" he gasped and flew back to the hall.

Jan was happily nibbling crisps and smiled up at him. Steve cast a glance at Liz who gave him the suggestion of a smile and turned away.

"Here's your lunch love," Jan put a pack of sandwiches in his hand.

"Thanks" replied Steve absentmindedly, then whispered "I want to talk to you but not here."

"What about? What's up?"

"Sh. Better wait until we are on our way home.

Jan was impatient. "But Steve---"

As her husband gave a slight nod in the direction of the adjoining stall, Jan felt the horrible feeling creeping back over her. Only minutes before she had been elated, and yet now, all the weight had returned. She knew that what Steve wanted to say would concern Liz, but she wasn't sure if she really wanted to listen. It would be distasteful. It would be obscene.

Jan crumpled her crisp packet and dropped it into the rubbish bag her mind racing. Liz had been at the side of her while Steve was away, so she could not have cornered him

"But where was she when I was gone?" The realization hit her.

"She was here, with him."

That afternoon was the longest Jan could ever remember spending.

Chapter 7

Not so for Tony Jennings. He packed every minute, and the days never seemed to be long enough to hold all his activities. Besides working with stamps, he was a keen collector, but true to form he only collected the best. His own albums, full of unmounted mint stamps were insured, and his expensive sets were housed in a bank deposit box. In contrast to such a delicate and detailed subject he was a fine handyman. In fact, he was as much at home with saw and chisel, as he was with tweezers and a magnifier. The display board which he was adjusting was all his own work although he was already contemplating ways to better it.

"This is showing signs of wear Brian" he spoke without lifting his eyes.

"Not surprising "came the reply "with all the knocking about it gets, especially on tour."

"Hmmm" Tony wished that Brian would not be quite so heavy handed with things that he did not consider carried a price tag.

"I'll just go and see about that Tudor Watermark set." Brian was already round the front of the stand and heading off in the direction of Bert.

"See you in half an hour" Tony still did not look up, not expecting a reply, which was just as well as Brian was intent on his objective.

Nora looked up as Brian approached. "Hello Brian, a bit slow this afternoon."

"Yes, I told Tony I didn't expect it would be very clever. Oh Bert, have you got that Tudor set?"

"Well if you lads are going to be here, I'm going for a walk round". Nora lifted herself with some effort, from her chair. "I'm a bit stiff."

"All right" Bert moved to let her pass, "Come round the back Brian." and the two heads inclined to study the prospective transaction.

As Nora wandered slowly around the various stalls, having a word with one or two of the other women, she had to admit, she wasn't feeling at her best. Come to think of it, she had not felt too good for some time.

"I ought to go and see Dr. Hodges, but he'll only say it's my age." Most things had been put down to her age for the last twenty five years, so Nora was not too happy about the prospect of wasting an hour or so for nothing. Her doctor had still not adopted an appointment system, so she would have to wait her turn in the queue. Supposing he wanted to examine her? What if she had to go to hospital? She let her hand rest on a nearby table to steady herself.

Liz looked up. "Feeling a bit groggy?"

"I'll be all right in a minute, thank you."

Jan appeared at her side. "Would you like to sit down for a moment, Nora?"

"No, thank you, please don't make a fuss, but just walk back to my stall with me would you?"

"Of course." and the two slowly strolled towards the door.

Liz slowly turned her head towards Steve. He felt her gaze boring into him and swung round to face her.

"Just what do you think you are playing at?"

"Playing? Oh I am not playing Steve. I never play."

The deadly earnest expression on her face and the tone of her voice left Steve in no doubt.

"I know your little game, you're a bloody queer, but you're versatile too. You've had a go at Jan, and don't deny it, and now you are trying it on with me. Well, it won't work." His voice although not more than a whisper, held the force of his anger.

Her eyes narrowed to slits. "Trying it on? When I want something, I get it."

She swung away and left the last statement ringing in his ears as Jan came hurrying back.

"We've sat her down, but she doesn't seem very well to me," a worried frown spread over her face.

"Who?"

"Why, Nora of course."

"Oh yes, is Bert taking her home then?"

Jan nodded. "It isn't very busy so he thought they would make an early day of it."

"I shouldn't mind doing the same, oh here's Tony" and he broke off to pay the stall rent.

"Done all right?" Tony took the money and immediately entered it on his clipboard.

"This morning was good, so can't grumble."

Tony smiled. "I think most are in the same boat today, oh, I'll ring you about the tour, I've got your number."

"Fine" Steve smiled in return. His face dropped as he turned to Jan. "Let's go."

She didn't need telling twice and started to gather up the books and smaller items whilst Steve busied himself with the heavier boxes.

"Going so soon?" Liz sounded smug.

"Yes, we've had enough for today." Jan would have preferred not to answer at all, but that would have been rather pointed.

"Steve gone to get the car?" Liz was being persistent.

"Why doesn't she shut up" Jan thought but answered with a curt "Yes."

"He thinks a lot of you doesn't he?"

"Of course."

"And such a fine body, but then you're not badly put together are you Jan?"

"Liz---"

"You make a fine couple." This statement had a ring of finality about it as Liz gave the other woman a short condescending smile.

It was with somewhat bewildered feelings that the Masters packed their car. Liz could almost have a softness about her, but it was the softness of a cat's gentle paw, that hid the lethal talons.

Giles was actually working. He had made a sale. It was amazing what satisfaction could do for a man. Not that he hadn't been satisfied the night before, but he was certain of his enjoyment tonight. That fact was assured when Barbie had entered the room that morning. She headed straight for Giles.

"I was hoping you would be here." she beamed. "Mummy and Daddy are away this weekend, and I have the house all to myself."

Barbie was class. Spoilt, but definitely Giles' type. She had only one fault. She was what Giles referred to as a 'Cling-on'. While he liked more than his share of enjoyment, he wanted none of the ties. Love them and leave them could have been written especially for him. Barbie was obviously looking for a catch, but having fun along the route, and it would have been the case of Barbie Foreman long ago if she had had her way.

But she was good for the night, and Giles was not going to turn down a chance like that. Comfort, willing bird, what more could a man ask. Anyway, he was doing her a favour. She wanted him, and some other, he did not quite know who, poor young lady would have to forego his attentions whilst he kept Barbie happy.

There was no need to note her address, he had been many times before, and with the promise of a meal as soon as he had finished the fair, he settled back, preened himself, and dwelt on the pleasures to come.

"Did you get that set off Bert?" Tony enquired as he and Brian packed up.

"Yes, I had to pay a bit more than I wanted, but I've got a customer for it."

"Oh good."

"I'm off tomorrow," Brian paused "so I shall have to go and unload tonight."

"I might have a day later in the week." Tony spoke as he worked. "Fred is fine on his own."

"He's still with us then," Brian sounded surprised. "I heard he was going out on his own."

"That was only speculation Brian, so don't mention it to anybody else. No, he is happy with us, and staying."

"Goodbye for now" The female tone broke into the conversation.

Both men turned to see Liz towing her trolley, absolutely laden with her belongings.

"Can you manage?" Brian started towards her.

"Would you be good enough to assist me to the car?" Liz almost purred her request.

Tony could not help thinking that Liz was quite capable, and only asked for help because it suited her purpose, which wasn't far wrong. Alone with Brian in the car park, Liz took full advantage of the situation. As they lifted boxes, her hand gently brushed various parts of the man's anatomy in such a seemingly accidental way, although every action was carefully manoeuvred. With Brian's very dull sex life, this was having a very pleasant effect on him and he was becoming aware of feelings he had long forgotten. Somehow, the pleasure was mixed with the uneasy feeling he had experienced the day before.

He gulped. "What are you doing to me?"

"I am doing nothing. You are doing it yourself. Men have vivid imaginations."

At which point she slammed the car boot, jumped into the driving seat and sped away. Brian stood alone, wondering. Was it his imagination? Perhaps it was his age. Funny things happened to men in their fifties didn't they? But he had not had a go at Liz. Had he? His mind racing in turmoil, he made his way slowly back to the room.

Chapter 8

The drone of the car engine could often have a soothing effect, whereas now it seemed to echo in every part of Nora's body.

"You'll have to stop for a while Bert, I can't make it home without a break."

Taking a quick glance at his wife, Bert noticed most of her colour had drained.

"There's a lay-by, I'll pull in." Bert swung off the road and stopped under the trees. Being early May, everything was looking fresh, but there was still quite a nip in the air. Nora laboriously wound down the window, and welcomed the cool breeze as it met her face.

"Mind not get cold" Bert shivered as he spoke. Then after a pause "Got one of your heads?"

The answer was not much more than a heavily breathed "Yes."

Bert thought for a moment then said, "Do you think these fairs could be getting a bit much for you?"

If Nora had felt better she would have given him a piece of her mind, instead she said quietly "I'm just a bit under the weather, that's all."

"Go and see the doc then."

"I might."

Bert grunted, "Do you feel like moving on? It's not far to home."

"All right." Nora wound up the window,

As they rejoined the road Bert said "What about the tour?"

After a pause Nora asked "What about it?"

"Well, I was only thinking" Bert began to wish he hadn't "that if you feel like this, I mean would it be a bit much, um, if you ---"

Nora settled the question "I will be all right Bert. I'll go and see Dr. Hodges next week before we go. Anyway I was looking forward to it. Do us good. Make a nice change."

Bert knew very well it was no good pursuing the subject, so he settled back to getting her home as quickly as possible. It was therefore a relief to both when the front gate appeared in front of them. As Nora got out of the car she paused.

"That Liz asked if I was all right."

Bert looked puzzled. "So?"

"When Jan brought me back, Liz had asked was I all right."

"That was nice of her" Bert did not see any particular significance.

"Exactly." and she let herself in the front door while Bert put the car in the garage.

Nora pondered. About Liz. About the tour. About her health. Had she only known what fate held in store for her.

"You said we would talk on the way home Steve." Jan was a little impatient as they travelled along the motorway.

"I know I did, but I'd rather talk when I can give you my full attention angel, so let's wait until we get home. O.K.?"

"If you say so Steve. If you would rather concentrate on driving, but you will tell me?"

"I've said so." the reply was almost curt.

They exchanged few words until they arrived home and were eating the quick meal Jan had prepared.

"Right." Steve began. "We have never had any secrets Jan, and I don't want to start now. I will be honest with you and I expect you to be the same with me. "

Jan paled a little.

"Is that understood?" Steve was insistent before going on.

"Yes of course."

"Now, I want you to tell me exactly what happened yesterday."

"Happened?" Jan was wondering just how much Steve already knew.

"Well, I didn't pay too much attention to what you said yesterday. I thought you were imagining things, but after you had gone to the ladies I noticed Liz was missing. Then I got busy but you seemed to be gone ages, and when you came back you were very quiet. And then last night------, tell me, did she do anything to you?"

Jan hesitated, so Steve encouraged "Come on angel, I want you to tell me, because I've got something to tell you afterwards."

Jan explained all that had happened, gathering confidence as she went on.

"Why didn't you say when we came home?" Steve's eyes showed anger.

"I thought you would laugh at me again, but oh Steve, I felt so dirty, and when you came to me in the shower, it all came back. It didn't seem right for you to touch me. Please don't ask me to explain it, I can't." Jan was almost sobbing.

Steve slipped his arm around her, led her to the settee, and went on to relate the event earlier in the day. Now it was Jan's turn to be angry. Steve concluded by saying, "I confronted her and accused her of having a go at you and she didn't deny it, so I knew something had happened."

Jan still looked aghast. "But she was able to get you going, that's horrible."

"Not in that way, she didn't actually turn me on, well not the same way you do."

"But she still got you aroused."

"Yes" Steve had to admit it "But I felt revulsion for her. Like you did yesterday" he reminder her.

"She didn't touch me" Jan played with a stray cotton on Steve's shirt.

"She didn't touch me either, but that woman's got power."

"And we know what she uses it for."

Steve shifted his position. "She is probably very frustrated."

"You'll be feeling sorry for her next."

"No, of course I won't. I'm just trying to find a reason for why she does what she does."

Jan thought for a moment. "What are we going to do?"

"What can we do? What has she actually done? I can't say to Brian and Tony, don't let Liz come to the fairs, she'd seduced my wife and myself but she has only looked at us."

Jan smirked "It sounds daft when you say it like that, and don't forget you laughed at me first."

"I know" Steve looked worried, "but I have to admit it is not so funny when it happens to you."

"Do we have to wait for it to happen to everyone before we can do anything?" Jan's retort was loaded with sarcasm.

"Surely" Steve brightened, "If we stick together against her, she wouldn't be able to succeed."

"How do you mean exactly?"

"Well," he was eager now "if she starts, we tell her she is a dirty old cow or something and flatten her ego, that should do it."

"It's possible" then Jan caught Steve's mischievous smile and said "You're just trying to make me laugh it off" and hit him playfully with a cushion.

"Worth a try" Steve stood up "We won't see her for a week, so we can get her out of our systems."

"How can one person have so much effect on someone else?" Jan moved to the table and gathered the plates as she spoke. She was feeling much easier in her mind since their chat.

"I don't know, but I think we've got her licked now angel, she can't fight the two of us" and Steve helped his wife into the kitchen with the usual little pat.

"It's when she catches us alone." Jan started to wash up.

"We know what to do now" Steve wanted no further discussion "We agreed, right?"

The reply came after a slight pause.

"Tell her to splodge off!"

Giles swung his vivid blue estate car into the gravel drive and knowingly parked round the side of the house, out of sight of the road.

He quickly entered by a side door and thought, "This really isn't a bad little place."

Standing in its own grounds, this was a rather splendid four bedroomed house, none of the rooms being small. The whole building, its contents and decor positively reeked of money. You could smell it. It was almost feasible to believe it manufactured the stuff. Oh yes. This was more Giles' cup of tea. As he paused in the well appointed kitchen, he felt the bonds springing up to trap him again.

"Perfect," he thought, "for a visit."

"Giles, is that you?" The tinkling voice floated down the hall.

"Don't tell me you were expecting a string of young gentlemen!" The door burst open and Barbie appeared. Without hesitation she ran into the now open arms.

"No of course not, silly, I just wanted to make sure it wasn't an intruder."

"Oh, I am sure a burglar would have answered," Giles laughed.

"Come on, let's eat, you must be famished."

"I'm certainly hungry, but who's talking about food?" Giles held the wriggling, laughing youthful form in an unyielding bear hug.

"But you must eat first, I've spent ages preparing your favourite."

"And just what did you have in mind for desert Miss Bessinger-Smythe?" Giles smothered her face in quick kisses.

"Why, me of course. Oh Giles, why has it been so long, you know I miss you madly, and you don't even 'phone." The pretty mouth dropped into a rather childish pout.

"Work, work, my pretty one." Giles felt the situation closing in. Change the subject. Good idea.

"Now, what did you say you had been cooking, beans on toast was it?"

The smile returned immediately. "Heavens no, silly. I told you it was your favourite. I've made you a mousaka."

"Mousaka," Giles kissed his fingers into the air. "Tell me more."

"Well, I was going to do a lemon soufflé, but changed my mind at the last minute, and I've done a cheesecake."

"Oh." "Doesn't sound like one of Barbie's specials" thought Giles to himself.

"With Tia Maria in it." she added.

"Ah, that sounds delightful," and he gesticulated for her to lead the way into the dining room.

Barbie had excelled herself. They both enjoyed a most delicious meal, and Giles mused over his coffee, "This girl can certainly cook -- as well."

"What are you thinking" Barbie had moved to the settee and spread herself across his lap.

"I neglect you something awful, I don't see you nearly enough," which was exactly his intention. Barbie's eyes brightened.

"Well, you know the answer to that darling, come more often, you know Mummy and Daddy are only too delighted to have you here, you can stay whenever you like." The words came tumbling out in her excitement.

"I'm so busy these days dear thing. It's all go, in fact I'm off on tour next week. Sad I know, but a chap's got to earn a crust of bread."

They chatted idly for a while, then Barbie ventured "You must be dead on your feet. Would you like to relax? We won't be disturbed. Like I said, Mummy and Daddy are away this weekend visiting my aunt. They won't be back until tomorrow night, so there's no one here but us."

"My dear girl that is music to a weary man that has been striving all day for a mere pittance."

Barbie stood up, pulled Giles by the hand and led him upstairs to her room.

"You've altered it" he stood in the doorway his eyes scanning the whole room.

"Yes, do you like it?"

Definitely a young ladies' room.

"Looks like you favour pink. Everything is pink."

"Daddy said I could have it how I wanted. It's all new, must have cost him a packet. Isn't he a poppet?"

"He certainly is," Giles breathed trying not to feel as though he had just been swallowed whole by a flamingo.

He drew the girl into his arms and they stood locked in an embrace for several moments, exchanging kisses, until they gradually moved towards the bed. As their mutual intentions were an understood part of the evening, both wasted no time in shedding their clothes and sliding happily between the sheets. Pink satin sheets. After a few moments of the usual petting, whispering of sweet nothings and giggles, Barbie looked up into Giles face and drawled "Giles?"

There was a warning bell ringing in his brain.

Young Mr. Foreman's senses were on full alert. "She is going to start being possessive again" flashed through his mind but whispered in her ear "Don't speak, just let me look at you."

"No Giles, do listen sweetie," she was putting on the little girl imploring with Daddy look. Giles could see how she wound her father round her little finger when she wanted something.

Not to be put off she continued "You know you said you were doing a tour next week?"

"Wait for it" Giles could see what was forming in her devious little mind. "Yes."

"Well, it's obvious. I'll come with you." This thought, although elating the girl was just as quickly deflating her bedmate.

"That is really going to cramp my style." Giles had to think fast or his freedom was in jeopardy. He looked with fake disappointment and explained "You know there is nothing I would like better my pet,"

"Well then" cut in Barbie" that's settled then."

"As I was about to explain, the rooms are already booked, and we have to keep the numbers to the minimum, and I may have to travel with someone else, cost cutting. You do understand, don't you my dear girl?"

Barbie snuggled down "Of course," but was already formulating her own little plan. What a lovely surprise she would give him. With smug satisfaction, Giles let his hand roam over her ripe body, thinking how well he had handled what could well have been a very tricky situation. He leaned across her to extinguish the small pink bedside lamp, and they both slipped into their own little world.

Chapter 9

Tony Jennings unlocked the shop in Charles Street and unloaded the stands and boxes of books. Within minutes his salesman, Fred arrived.

"Perfect timing," Tony knew he could trust Fred to put everything in place, whilst he opened the mail.

"Good week end Tony?" the salesman's smile was bright and his manner willing.

"Not bad, we had a few good buys, and sold quite a bit we had hanging about for ages. We need to make up some more bags of kiloware."

"I'll get straight on to it when I've done this." Fred busied himself with the task in hand.

As Tony was flicking through his mail, he picked up the telephone and dialled the number of the Main Street shop. It did not take John the manager, long to answer. The two exchanged news of sales both at the shops and the fairs. John didn't travel well and so it suited him to stay put and be an anchor man for the other two shops when Brian and Tony were away. All realised that the tours and fairs were essential to buy in new stock and create new postal customers. You had to go to people. They would come to you to sell, but only if you were near enough to them. Sometimes on tour, a possible vendor would not want, or be able to bring their collections to a fair, but would wish the dealer to visit them afterwards to value and make an offer.

"Could you spare Martin next week John?" Tony was eager to get the details of the tour finalised.

"Fine by me. Let me just check with him Tony." a slight pause, "Yes that is all right, will you give him the details later in the week?"

"Will do, but tell him we leave early Monday morning and we will be back sometime Friday. He'll need to let his Mum know."

"I'll do that. Thanks. Bye."

Martin Smith was a shy quiet lad. Nobody could say they either liked or disliked him. He did as he was told, and could at any time have left a room, and returned without anyone being any the wiser. He lived with his mother, a widow, and although he was no trouble, he was also not a very good companion. Since passing his driving test, he had bought a cheap little car, and was able to take her shopping, which he did with no complaint, but as soon as they arrived home, he would bury his face in a book, and barely utter a sound.

"Strange boy," she would think, "not a bit like his father. Perhaps he misses him. No, he has always been the same. At school he didn't mix much with the other lads." But she was nevertheless grateful to have him around. Life would have been very lonely for her without him.

"So," John's voice startled him. "You are going on the tour?"

"Yes."

"You should enjoy it."

"Yes."

"Tony says they are leaving first thing Monday, he usually loads up the night before if they haven't got a fair Sunday."

"Oh."

"You will be coming back Friday, so you can tell your Mum."

"Thank you. Will I need any money?"

"Well, we pay for your hotel rooms and your evening meals, but if you want anything during the day I should take a bit for that." John almost felt sorry for him. "I bet he has to watch the pennies." he thought kindly.

Liz was feeling very pleased with herself. Steve was going to prove easier than she imagined. Pity really, she liked a challenge, always aiming to achieve the impossible. But he was putting up quite a good fight, trying to persuade her that it was only Jan for him, when all the time he was hers for the picking. She would continue to give the other males something to think of, the reason behind this was to put them all in the same position, so that one could not, or would not dare complain about her. Therefore if Steve was to confide in say, Brian he would not admit how he had felt. That still left Bert, not very attractive but a small enough sacrifice when she considered her goal. Giles, well he would not need any pushing. Tony, not too hopeful, but he was a man, and as yet no man had been able to resist her uncanny powers. And there were ways, when you knew how.

Her mind turned to the tour. The main objective, apart from making the final kill for Steve, would have to be getting Jan out of the way. The elusive smile appeared. Strange that Nora felt unwell right near her stall, and Jan had to help her. How very opportune. But as Liz would have verified, fate often needs a little push, and she was about to give it one almighty shove.

Nora sat in the waiting room of Dr. Hodges surgery, already regretting the visit. When her turn eventually came, she was eager to get it over with, than go into great lengths of her symptoms. After the allotted time per patient, approximately five minutes, she made her way back to the car and Bert.

"Well?" asked Bert as she climbed in clutching a prescription.

"Give me chance to get in." At least her spirit was not daunted. "I've got blood pressure."

"I should hope you have." Bert sniffed, "Be in a poor way without it you would."

"What are you talking about?" Nora had missed the point.

"Everyone has blood pressure love, is your's high or low?"

"Well high of course, nearly went out the top of his machine. I didn't know you could have low blood pressure. Can you stop at the chemist? I've got to get some pills."

"Of course," Bert was relieved she had been at last, he hadn't been happy with her state of health, but now at least he could put a name to it.

"Probably what makes you a bit edgy." He would have liked to say cantankerous, but through experience thought before he spoke.

"Edgy? When am I ever edgy as you call it?"

"When you are not well love, here is the chemist" he remarked with relief.

When Nora returned with her tablets she said "Dr. Hodges was saying he hadn't seen you for a while."

"What's strange about that?" Bert brushed the remark aside.

"They are thinking of starting a well-person clinic soon. You know, you're not ill but they check all your vital things over."

"Long time since my vital things were examined," beamed Bert.

"I do hope you are not going to be coarse." Nora was not amused. "There is no point in talking to you when you are in that mood."

"Whoops." Bert drove home in silence.

As the week slipped by, Steve and Jan returned to their normal relaxed loving relationship, all thoughts of Liz being pushed further into the background.

"If only we could never see her again, everything would be all right." Jan thought to herself as she made the bed. Their bed. Their haven of trust and affection, where any suggestion of that woman was unwelcome. Steve did not like to even mention 'her', so Jan mused to herself but did not voice her feelings. Why upset Steve when he only wanted her. He did not want Liz. The thought of her effect on him still niggled in the back of her mind, but she brushed it aside. "He is mine, all mine, not yours madam, and never will be." She felt the venom rise. "I am a match for you." but even with the show of bravado, Jan knew deep inside, that she could never equal the powers of Ms. Niebur.

"Where are you angel?"

Steve's cheery call snapped her out of herself.

"Coming." She flew down the stairs and into his arms. "Good day?"

"Known better. What does it matter, I'm home now. We've got nothing planned for tonight have we, I feel like just relaxing and watching that film on the telly".

"Suits me." "The more I have him to myself the better." thought Jan, "get her out of his system, for good."

"I've got a bit of marking to do, but it won't take long. What's for dinner? Smells delicious." Steve sniffed the air appreciatively.

"Only shepherds pie-----"

"What do you mean only," he grabbed Jan again, "you know it's my favourite, next to you. Think I'll eat you first."

Jan struggled free and her husband chased her playfully around the room until they both fell on to the settee laughing, kissing, hugging, loving.

Suddenly, they were not laughing. The playfulness turned quickly to passion as Steve kissed Jan so fiercely and she responded with a willingness she could not control. They rolled to the floor, and within a moment were joined, body and mind together, with a feeling that surpassed anything they had ever experienced.

They lay there for, what seemed an eternity, and when Jan looked into Steve's eyes, she saw they were wet.

"Steve--"she began.

"Thank you, my angel, thank you." his voice was choked with emotion.

"What ever is the matter, I have never seen you like this." Jan was somewhat bewildered.

"I don't know, I have never felt so good, you have never been so good." He could not express his feelings in words, so he held her close and whispered "My angel, my precious angel."

When they had both returned to normal, Jan could not control the ideas which flooded her mind.

"Why had they not felt like this before? Why was it so good? Why was it different?"

An uneasy sensation crept into the pit of her stomach as she recalled Liz's remark "You make a lovely couple."

"No. There is no way that pervert could have any effect on our lovemaking." and she pushed the idea aside, as if she were pushing the woman herself.

After they had washed, the couple enjoyed their meal, and although the conversation was a little sparse, the Masters exchanged loving glances and smiles that hid an inner torment in both.

Chapter 10

The crisp spring Monday morning saw the soon to be convoy departing from their various places of abode. Brian and Tony had decided to take both cars, therefore being able to carry as much stock as possible, Brian to take the fair advertising boards, and Martin to travel with Tony.

Bert and Nora had made an earlier start, so that Nora did not have to rush about, and could have a break at the pre arranged service area, whilst waiting for the others. Brian and Tony arrived followed soon after by Liz, who remained in her car and made no attempt to chat with the others.

Steve and Jan swung in alongside Tony.

"Thought we would be last," Steve called as his lowered his window "had a slight delay, sorry."

"You are O.K. we are in good time, except for you know who," Tony cast a view over the assembled company.

"Giles." Steve had half hoped the woman in black, as he now called Liz to prevent using her name, had changed her mind. "No such luck." There she sat, alone, composed, and looking extremely self satisfied.

With a screech of tyres, Giles arrived in a blue streak as though he had made a grand stage appearance.

Tony went straight to the drivers' window.

"If you are ready, we will be off."

Giles cut in "Ready as I will ever be."

"As I was about to say," Tony was determined to be heard, "could you try and keep with the rest of us this time. I know you like to put your foot down, but we don't want that problem again of having to find you when we get there."

"Yes sir." Giles gave a mock salute and thought "Who does he think he is, but then I suppose some minion has to do the menial tasks."

As Tony returned to his vehicle he wished he could take that young man down a peg or two, but why waste energy on his sort. They always got their comeuppance eventually.

The small company departed. They would travel to Weymouth today and book into the hotel at their leisure, which meant they would be suitable refreshed before the fair there on Tuesday. It also gave Tony plenty of time to check final arrangements for the hall they had hired, and give it his once over.

After they had all packed up, they would all travel on to Poole, just along the coast, stay there on Tuesday night, ready for the Wednesday venue. The same would then happen ready for Bournemouth on Thursday, with everyone returning on Friday. Nobody relished the idea of driving back on Thursday night, with the exception of Tony, but he considered that he would have to make sure everything was cleared up and settled, and he couldn't trust Brian to take care of it, so he would fall in with the rest. There was always the possibility of having to go out to a collection anyway. The two men had considered the closeness of venues, as Poole was almost round the corner from Bournemouth. The fit could walk it. But they had decided to risk it, with the hope of catching early holiday makers, perhaps even foreigners arriving on the ferries.

"It's like having two bites of the cherry," Brian had said thinking it had all been his idea in the first place.

So the plan for the week was set into operation.

"I'm glad we are well wrapped up," Jan pulled her coat around her, "but isn't this just beautiful?"

Steve cuddled her towards him, as they stood together at the Nothe Fort, the clean white buildings of Weymouth to one side, and the naval base at Portland to the other.

"Heaven." Then squeezing her to him he said "Shall we take a drive over to Portland, we can still admire the scenery, but it would be warmer."

"Anywhere, as long as we are together, alone."

It was a lovely evening, but the warmth had yet to make itself felt, and the breeze from the sea seemed to catch them from all quarters.

As they returned to the car Steve said "I think there is a prison on the top of Portland, but I'm not sure if it is still in use."

"I don't mind if we don't find out." Jan laughed with an ease that was very welcome.

As they pulled out of the parking space, they saw Nora and Bert coming in. Steve slowed the car to a halt. Both drivers wound down their windows as they drew alongside.

"A bit chilly up there, take care both of you." Steve was aware of Nora's recent little funny turn.

Bert opened his mouth to reply, but it was Nora who said "Thank you Steve, but I'll probably just sit in the car while Bert goes for a stroll." and with a nod to Jan they occupied the parking place just vacated.

Brian and Tony were going over the table plans for the following day.

"Where have we put Liz?" Brian tried to make the remark as casual as possible.

"Why? What difference does it make? There." and Tony jabbed a finger on the paper set out in front of them.

"Oh nothing. and where is Giles?" Brian tried to cover up his enquiry with another seemingly innocent one.

Tony grunted to himself. It was just like his colleague to stick his nose in when all the work was done.

"Next to us. Now is there anything else?" but without waiting for a reply he folded the sheet of paper and put it into his briefcase.

Giles had gone out. Somewhere. Anywhere. Nobody had the slightest interest in what he did or with whom. Except maybe one person.

Liz viewed her temporary room with alien feelings. She much preferred to be in her own setting, with her own inanimate companions. Granted, she had brought a few special items with her, things that helped her to meditate and concentrate her thoughts on the target she had set herself. She fondled a pair of tweezers and a pack of showguard mounts. Not hers, his. They had very conveniently slid from his stall to hers when they stood alongside. The intention had not been to steal, she did not need to, the purpose was to possess, firstly something belonging to him, and then him. She slid the items lovingly down the length of her torso, and became engrossed in her efforts towards achieving her goal.

"It will not be long now." The room gradually faded as she felt a surge of power engulf her body and with closed eyes she projected her mind out and beyond.

Martin did not want to go out. He had brought some books with him and now sat alone in his room. A gently tap on the door made him jump. He carefully opened the door, and peered out.

"You O.K.?" Tony stood alone. "It's just that we haven't seen you all evening, and we are going down to the bar for a drink. Want to join us?"

"No, no, but thanks all the same. I am all right, I'm reading."

"Suit yourself, but you know where we are if you change your mind," Tony called over his shoulder as he retreated down the hallway.

Martin scurried back to his book, grateful that Tony had not persisted with the invitation, but then Tony was like that, which was why Martin liked him. More than he could say for Giles.

The fairs at Weymouth and Poole passed without special significance. There was the usual little trickle of people uttering comments like, "We chucked stuff like that away," and "I've got loads of those at home," which prompted unheard replies of "You don't want these then."

As it was getting towards the end of May, many people were looking to sell rather than buy. With the holidays looming, most wanted spending money, and would go through their collections to rid themselves of duplicates and surplus stock. It was, from a dealers' point of view, a lean time for taking money, but you needed to have plenty to spend because this was when the stock would be available. In theory it sounded perfect but life is not always that kind. Many would agree that when you have had a good fair and money in your pocket, no good material appeared for sale. Likewise, if you were a bit skint, everything came flooding your way, stuff you just could not let go because you could make a good profit on it, so you beg, borrow or whatever, on the chance of a good return later.

    They wasted no time in packing up after Poole, all of the dealers looking forward to the short trip to Bournemouth and a hearty meal. All were feeling tired, mainly from the lack of activity, rather than the hectic pace of the week end venues. There was no question as to which they preferred, but most made the best of it and enjoyed the sea air as and when they could.

Chapter 11

The hotel was a modern affair on the outskirts of the town, with long corridors of guest rooms on the first floor, all having en suite bathrooms, and facilities for making hot drinks. The ground floor was given entirely to the usual reception area, restaurant, bar, lounge, and many function rooms, one of which had been hired for Thursdays fair.

The assembled group awaited Tony's arrival, as it was the accepted thing that he took charge wherever they went, and as he did the job in his normal brilliant manner, everyone was reassured that everything would be right. If it wasn't, he would see to it. Tony appeared with Martin scurrying behind him like a shadow.

"Right, is everyone here?" he quickly counted the heads, and without waiting for a reply continued, "Good, let's get checked in, and then we can all eat." He strode to the reception desk, and was soon organising the signing in.

"As there are quite a few of you, I'm afraid we haven't been able to put you all next to each other," the smart young receptionist apologised.

"Do we all have a room as booked?" Tony's smile was fixed, but his manner said no nonsense.

"Oh yes."

"Then we do not have a problem. Who's first?" Tony was eager to get everyone settled.

The young lady consulted her book and selected a number of keys.

"Mr. Smith? she looked up smiling as Martin stepped forward.

"Number twenty three sir, up the stairs, or you can take the lift, turn right and your room is on the left."

Martin stood there, embarrassed to leave first. Steve noticed and whispered, "We may as well all go together when we all have our keys."

A look of relief spread over Martin's face. "Yes, good idea."

"Mr. Foreman, you are next door to Mr. Smith in number twenty five."

"Thank you dear thing," as Giles took the key he lingered over the outstretched hand.

"Yes, yes, we don't want to be here all night," Tony was still supervising.

"Mrs. Niebur, oh sorry is it Miss," the receptionist looked at Liz with interest.

"Ms."

"Oh I am sorry Ms. Niebur, you are in number twenty four, opposite the two young gentlemen." Her voice slipped into a whisper as she caught Liz's penetrating stare. As she took her key she let her gaze slip over both men. Giles gave a nonchalant shrug and turned away, while Martin visibly trembled.

"Poor beggar won't stand a chance if she gets her claws into him." Bert was amused by the scene and whispered to Brian.

"Mr. Dakin" Brian was rather glad of the interruption. "This is where you spread out a bit. You are in number thirty."

"Not far from Liz" he thought, "I wonder if that is a good thing or a bad thing."

"Mr. Jennings, oh yes that's you isn't it, you did the booking."

"She must have been blessed with more than one brain cell" Tony gave a vestige of a smile took his key and stood back.

"Number thirty three"

"Yes, thank you so I see."

"Mr. and Mrs. Masters, you are in number thirty eight, and Mr. and Mrs. Dennis, number forty five."

Brian, Martin and Liz had already made their way up and were intent on getting settled in for the two night's stay, when the lift returned. Nora was sitting down on a nearby easy chair, and Giles was busy trying to chat up the receptionist, without much luck, so Tony, Steve and Jan took the next trip.

"Come along Nora, you can't sit there all night." Bert picked up the bags.

They made their way along to the lift, and were just boarding when Giles came rushing over, "Wait for a little one."

The corridor was empty when they got to the first floor, all of the others now engrossed in settling in.

"Well here I am," Giles opened his door. "Oh twin beds, I must have ordered a double." His mock surprise did not fool either of the older couple." "Not much privacy with the others being so close, I'll have to keep the sound down" he cockily chuckled to himself.

"Well, how far are we?" Nora's voice made him realise he hadn't closed the door. A burst of inspiration struck him.

"Hang on here a minute Nora, if yours is very far away, we'll swap if you like, I'll go and check it out. Have you got the key?"

"We'll all go." Nora wasn't at all sure of his motive.

"Leave the bags here," suggested Bert, "no need to carry them if we are staying here."

As they opened the door of number forty five, the first thing they all noticed was the double bed, although for different reasons.

"It is a bit far to keep walking Giles, and you are a lot younger, would you mind then?"

Nora looked at Bert who nodded in agreement.

"Think nothing of it Nora. Now, I'll just come back with you to pick up my things which I left in my, I mean your room."

"What about the hotel staff?" Bert asked as they walked back.

"What about them, nothing to do with them old boy as long as we pay."

"No, what I mean is they have our room numbers on record, in case of fire or something, I think we should let them know we have changed."

"Leave it to me" Giles wanted no problems, "I'll nip down when I've unpacked and amend it, no need for you to have the bother."

"You will do it?" Nora sank onto the nearest bed as they entered the room.

"Consider it done" and he made his way back to his new love nest.

As he swung his bag in sheer elation, Giles congratulated himself. "Yes" he pushed the word out as he punched the air. "Some little filly is going to be very grateful. I wonder who it will be this time."

The next morning every one was feeling a little jaded, and in some ways glad this was the last venue. Nora was determined not to overdo it, and if things weren't too busy she might have a little stroll later if the weather was nice. Bert could manage.

Tony and Martin enjoyed an early breakfast, and made their way to the hall allotted to them. No doubt Brian would join them shortly.

"Lighting could be better" Tony frowned," you see why we carry so much of our own."

"All the hotels are the same aren't they," Martin said, "low ceilings and subdued light."

"Some people might just be grateful for that, but I like to see what I am doing, especially what I am buying."

"Nice carpet." Martin felt easy in Tony's company, and was more talkative to him than any of the others. "Looks new."

"Yes" Tony looked down, "cost a bit I should think."

The two men happily exchanged comments as they set up their own stand. The others slowly filtered in, spread themselves out and set up.

Martin watched as Giles carelessly tossed things on to the table in front of him. It did not seem to matter where they landed or how they looked. He did not like this person. His eyes moved back to where he sat. Everything was in place. Stock books open, the display board freshly re-stocked with postal history, and the flop-over stands full of first day covers, presentation packs, and PHQs, the postcards of each stamp issue, both mint and used. The packs of kiloware, stamps saved for charities and sold to the dealers were weighed and priced and neatly placed in a basket. He admired Tony's attitude and conscientiousness, and could not help but make comparisons with Brian's relaxed approach.

His attention was suddenly drawn to the doorway. Barbie looked straight at him, then turned her attention to Giles. Without invitation, she made for the back of his stall, found a chair and sat down, pushing her hold all between the boxes. Giles face was a picture. This was something he did not expect or want.

"What are you doing here?" he finally managed to blurt out.

"Darling, you don't seem pleased to see me." The familiar pout appeared.

"Surprised that's all."

She brightened, her spirits refusing to be squashed.

"I would have come yesterday" she bubbled "but something came up, so here I am, and guess what? I can stay with you until tomorrow, and then go back with you." If she was waiting for applause she would be disappointed.

Giles composed himself. This was not what he had in mind for tonight, and that trapped feeling was threatening.

"She's getting her claws in."

As he turned to answer he noticed she was giving Martin several sidelong glances, and the lad was returning them. "Could I offload her there?" was his first thought, but then "No, he wouldn't have a clue, wouldn't do for her, she liked more life in a body."

"Well that seems to be settled then." He hoped his voice sounded more casual than he felt inside.

"You had better book me in to stay." she certainly had it all figured out.

"Yes, I will see to it." The thought crossed his mind that he had not yet changed the room numbers at reception.

"I'll do both together, sometime" he thought to himself.

As the day drifted to a close, Jan was grateful that Liz seemed to have left them alone on this tour.

"She could really have made things unpleasant," she muttered to Steve.

"Forget her." Steve could not think of Liz without remembering the feelings she could muster and he did not want to discuss her with Jan.

Nora was looking forward to packing up. She had enjoyed herself but if she admitted it she had felt the effects and the strain of the last few days. Bert would only fuss if she said anything so it was best to take her pills and carry on.

Liz was getting ready for the kill. She was like a hungry lioness, but was not about to stay hungry. Events were about to lay her chance right in her lap, but with this woman, who could say how much was chance, and how much she engineered it.

Brian was tired. "I shall have a couple of days off when we get back" he told Tony "I'm always tired after a tour. You'll be around won't you?"

"Just as well," thought Tony "doesn't he think I get shattered at times?"

As if an invisible whistle had been blown, everyone started to pack up simultaneously. They were all ready for a relaxing evening before the journey home tomorrow. The hotel staff began hovering in their eagerness to clear the room. In the end they began to get in the way putting tables away while the dealers were trying to carry out their stock.

Tony eventually pounced on the nearest to him.

"If you would only let us get cleared, you would have an easier task with the room vacated." he felt his temper rising.

The staff member said offhandedly, "We have another booking in here at six, and we need you out as soon as possible."

"And I have paid for this room until five o'clock, it is now four forty five, and it is not my problem if you do not leave enough time between your bookings. Now, kindly leave or fetch me the manager." With much resentment they shuffled out muttering.

"Thank you" Tony called after them. "Now we can do our job and you can then do yours."

Chapter 12

The meal had been delicious, and everyone settled down to relax. Giles and Barbie had gone out, much to most people's relief. They could be quite an embarrassment, and the atmosphere lightened when they left. Martin decided he would like to go to his room and finish his book and disappeared immediately. The men all sat talking shop and probably a few other things judging by the laughter that rose from time to time. Nora and Jan sat in a corner on a very comfortable sofa.

"I could nod off," Nora was not far away from sleep and was in quite a happy frame of mind.

"Me too," yawned Jan. "Do you think anyone would notice?"

"Doubt it. Look at them, like a bunch of school boys." and she inclined her head towards the four as another burst of raucous laughter emitted.

"Bet that was a dirty one" thought Jan but kept it to herself.

Liz had slipped away to her room. Steve wondered where she had gone but said nothing. After a while Brian suggested a game of cards.

"Don't think they would like it in here" Tony was doubtful.

"My room then," Brian liked a game although he hardly ever won. Steve and Tony nodded but Bert said "Count me out, I'm feeling a bit weary lads."

"You O.K. Bert?" Steve asked as Bert rose to his feet.

"Yes, yes just a bit tired, I'll probably have an early night." So saying he made his way over to Nora and Jan.

"I'm going to have one of your headache tablets Nora, and have a lie down. You stay here and talk to Jan."

Both women enquired if he was feeling ill.

"No just a bit tired." and he turned and went to his room.

Martin eyed the glass of wine he had bought at the bar, and taken to the safety of his room.

"I just need the right moment,"

The hotel was considerably quieter than earlier in the day, and his ears adjusted to individual sounds. A slight shuffle in the corridor alerted his senses. He quietly slipped to the door and peeped out to see the door of number twenty five just closing.

"Perfect he thought, he's back, and I don't even care if she is in there with him. Even better."

He went back to the table, collected the glass of wine, and made his way to the room next door. He nearly spilled the wine as he was startled by the appearance of Liz, who eyed him rather searchingly.

"I - um "he flustered.

Liz said nothing.

"The waiter brought this to the wrong place, it must be for him." and he nodded in the direction of what he considered to be Giles' room.

"Stupid child, he doesn't even know they have swapped," but knowing Bert was in there, alone, gave her ample opportunity to pursue her little scheme.

"Give it to me, I'll see that he gets it," and she took the glass from his hand. "Run along now, there's a good boy." and she waited until he had disappeared.

Her gentle tap on the door was answered by a subdued "Come in."

She slid in and closed the door behind her.

Bert looked amazed. "Liz, I thought it was one of the lads. What do you want?"

Silently she put the wine on the bedside table and sat down beside him on the bed.

"Now you just rest," she eased him into a lying position on his back, and as her words flowed over his tired brain, he felt himself slowly drifting, floating away in an experience he had never before witnessed, certainly not with Nora! He was barely aware of Liz's hands as they manipulated his lower body until a pleasurable surge flowing through his whole being. The excitement was building in him like a volcano about to erupt. He was unable to stop her. He did not want to stop her. Suddenly, a tightness crept over his chest and he sat up as a searing pain ripped him apart. Liz rose to her feet, left the room and just made out a faint "Liz. For God's sake help me." as Bert clutched his chest the beads of sweat appearing on his face.

Nora's scream brought Jan running back to her. The two had decided to turn in and get some well deserved rest. Steve and Tony were just getting down to a hand of cards in Brian's room and all three came rushing out.

"What is it?" Jan was first at Nora's side.

"It's, it's... Bert," she was sobbing. Jan rushed to the bed. "Help me get him into a sitting position Steve."

"We'll do it," Tony moved Jan aside and called to Brian "Get an ambulance"

"I'll do it." Jan was already at the telephone. She called down to reception, explained the situation and they promised to call for an ambulance straight away. Brian was still hovering just outside, when Tony took charge in his usual manner.

"Getting a bit crowded in here, Bert needs to be quiet. Can you two manage?" he gave a knowing look to Steve who said "Yes, we will look after things here." and Tony shepherded Brian away.

"Will he be going to hospital?" Nora held Jan's hand for support.

"Just to see that he will be all right Nora, it's the best thing." Jan then turned to Steve, "I had better go with her."

"Oh would you Jan - "and Nora broke off and wept.

Steve was adamant. "Of course Jan, you must. Tell you what, you don't know how long you will be, so give me a call and I will fetch you back when you are ready." He looked towards Bert "May just keep you in old trooper," Bert nodded knowing full well he was right.

"You don't even know where the hospital is Steve, and we may be some time. We'll get a taxi." Jan thought it better for her husband to get to bed. She wasn't the only one on that wavelength.

The ambulance arrived with two able crew on board, and soon Bert was being carried on a chair with Nora and Jan close behind. Steve briefly straightened the room, picked up the key and locked the door behind him.

"I'll give it to Nora when she comes back," he thought "I'll wait up for Jan anyway, so no point in taking it to reception."

As he was about to return to Brian's room, Tony met him.

"How's Bert?"

"I reckon he'll be right as rain soon, but we will have to see when-_"

They were interrupted by a distraught Martin who suddenly appeared in front of them. "I didn't mean it. I've poisoned him, and why was he in Giles' room?"

Both men gave each other a quick glance and bundled Martin backwards into his room. The force made him fall on to the bed. The two immediately took positions either side of him.

"O.K. now, exactly what are you babbling on about?" Tony's manner was almost brutal.

Steve cut in. "Gently Tony, now Martin, take it slowly."

The tears were streaming down the young lad's face.

"I only wanted to teach him a lesson, I should never have done it."

"Done what?" Tony spat out the question.

"Put something in his drink, and now Bert's drank it not Giles and- and-"

"Wait a minute." Steve decided they had to get the full story. There was a lot more to this than met the eye.

"Now, start at the beginning, and tell us everything."

Martin looked searchingly from Steve to Tony, and when the latter nodded for him to continue, he began.

"I didn't want him to have her."

"Her?" Tony was lost already.

"Barbie."

"Not Giles' bit of, sorry, that Barbie." Steve picked his words

"Yes."

"Why, what is she to you?" Tony had the feeling this was going to be a long session.

"My cousin."

"Your cousin" rang out in unison.

"Her father is my uncle, he's done well for himself and, well, we aren't in their class anymore."

"The poor relations," Steve tried to help him along.

"Yes you could say that."

"But hang on a minute," Tony queried, "her name is what, something double barreled."

"Bessinger-Smythe. You see Harry Smith doesn't sound half so impressive as Henry Bessinger-Smythe does it?"

"Depends which side of the money you are on." Tony smiled briefly.

"Bessinger was Barbie's mother's maiden name, and the Smith became Smythe, and they changed it by deed poll."

"So where exactly does that leave you?" Steve was still trying to piece all this together. "You couldn't marry her, not if you are cousins."

"No, well I've always liked her a lot, I mean before she became so, well popular."

"Promiscuous is the word he is looking for" Tony thought to himself.

"I can't stand Giles, he is so self centred, and she could do a lot better than him, the family don't like him either."

Steve smiled, "If they treated me like the poor relations, I should take it as a smack in the eye to them if she did get Giles."

Tony could not help grinning in agreement. They both looked at Martin, but the remark was lost on him.

"So what about the drink?"

A knock came at the door. Tony opened it a fraction and saw Brian standing there.

"Oh here you are, I wondered where you had got to."

"Martin's a bit upset about poor old Bert, never seen anyone like that before. He'll be O.K. Steve and I are just having a chat with him."

Brian quite satisfied with the simplest of explanations sauntered back to his room.

Tony returned to the others. "Right. Before we have any further interruptions, tell us what you did."

"Honestly, I only wanted to make him look a fool in front of her, then she would go off him. So I put something in a drink and when I heard him come back I went to take it to him. Only it wasn't him, it was Bert." The lip started to quiver again.

"Didn't you know Giles had swapped rooms with Bert and Nora," Tony couldn't believe this, "Just about everyone else did."

"Of course he didn't, that is obvious now." Steve gave the lad a friendly smile and said "So you put something in the drink. What was it?"

"Laxative."

The two interrogators nearly choked with mirth and relief.

"You put laxative in a drink and you thought you had poisoned him. Take a few packets to do that. Give him the trots for a while, but,----" Steve could not contain himself and laughed out loud.

"I thought if he was sick or, well you know, the other, in front of Barbie, she would despise him."

"Of all the schoolboy pranks." Tony was now serious.

"But wait a minute, if you took him the drink, why didn't you notice it was Bert?"

"Oh, I didn't actually take it in."

A small groan escaped Tony's lips. "Then who for pities sake did?"

"Liz."

"What in creation did Liz take it in for?" That woman was into everything. Steve felt the old uneasiness coming back.

Martin looked a little sheepish. "Well, as I was going to the door with it, Liz came up and said she would take it in for me."

"Did she now?" Steve was already searching for the reason. Liz must have known it would be Bert, not Giles in there. She would not have missed that fact.

Tony jumped up. "The glass. If Bert didn't drink it all, there would be something left in the glass."

"You think of everything." Martin did not know whether to feel relief, or renewed fear.

Steve was on his feet and half way across the room. "I have the key, I'll go and see."

"Good man." Tony sat down with Martin and they eagerly awaited his return.

Within seconds Steve came back holding the almost full glass. He closed the door before speaking.

"How much more was there?" He showed the glass and contents to Martin.

"That's it, that's what there was." The anguish began to drain from his face.

Tony summed up. "So Bert did not drink any of it, and if he was taken ill, it was something completely different."

"Think it was his heart." Steve looked at the other two, held up the glass, and with a nod from Tony, went into the bathroom and flushed the contents down the toilet.

"What is he doing?" Martin was showing signs of strain again.

"In the circumstances I think the least said about this the better. And the fewer people who know the better. Right Steve?" he looked up as Steve rejoined them.

"But---"began Martin looking from one to the other.

Tony was going to reassure him if it took all night.

"Martin, you did a very silly juvenile thing, which luckily backfired. Even if, as you hoped, Giles had consumed the lot, it still would not have been the end of the world. And Bert did not touch any of it, and we all know where it has ended up, if not in its originally intended form."

Martin thought he knew what Tony meant. Steve smiled," It went straight down instead of through Giles first."

"Oh."

Tony said in a whisper. "That just leaves Liz."

"Do you think she knows anything?" Martin had not forgotten how her eyes went through him earlier.

"More to the point, did she do anything?" Steve thought better than to voice this and instead said, "Well, enough for tonight, young man, you had better get some sleep."

Tony added "And don't forget, keep it under your hat."

Chapter 13

Steve walked with Tony as far as his room, bid him "Goodnight" and paused. He looked towards his own room, then turned and felt drawn back along the corridor. He was almost outside Martin's door, when the door at the side of him silently opened.

"You took your time." Liz looked as though she was expecting him long ago .She continued almost in a whisper "I do not conduct my conversations at the door, come in."

Steve had no wish to attract attention either from Martin or anyone else, and he had a burning curiosity to know why she had entered number twenty five. Perhaps a chat might reveal all. Jan would be ages yet, knowing the hospitals, so where was the harm?

He stepped inside and Liz closed the door and locked it.

"I can only be a minute," even to Steve's ears it sounded a tame opener.

"We do not talk enough," she began.

"And whose fault is that, you do not communicate much with your fellow companions."

"That is mere idle chatter Steve," her voice was beginning to lull him again and she drew him towards the bed and they both sat down.

"I mean really talk," he was slipping under the spell of her hypnotic strains, and he was enjoying it.

"We should float on other plains," she pushed him backwards and he drew her on top of him, "away from this basic form." He wanted her. No, he needed her with such an insatiable desire that nothing could stop him. Although he did not understand himself, he was driven on by a power within him that he could not and would not fight.

"Liz, Liz."

"He is almost mine" she thought but continued to whisper, keeping him in the trance. She shed her clothes and with Steve's help, undressed him. She held him back until he was almost exploding with desire for her, then let him take her.

They lay entwined as the realisation hit him. He had made love to Liz. He had given her one. He tried to think of all the different ways to say it, some not too gentlemanly. The true facts hit him even harder. He had no feeling of revulsion, he had wanted to do it, and he had enjoyed it. She did not seem weird or strange to him now, but a goddess who made him feel every inch a man. He realised that the uneasy feelings that had plagued him over recent weeks, were in fact desire for her.

She smiled at him as she gently raised herself up above him. "I've got him now, for as long as I want." the thought should have added until I want some one else.

"I can't let you go now Liz" he was getting excited again as she sank down on to him.

"You think I don't know that?" she was working on him again.

He had no idea of time as he slipped once again into the pool of oblivion, just him and Liz.

When he finally came back to his senses, he looked at his watch and gasped.

"It's half past twelve." he panicked. Hurriedly throwing on his clothes, he just stopped as he passed the mirror to check on his appearance.

"Jan."

"Jan who?" Liz's tail was waving .He was hers now.

"Jan must be back." He unlocked the door and flew down the corridor. In his haste he tried to use Bert's key, then stood to compose himself before trying his own. His head was reeling as he opened the door, and relief flooded in as he viewed the empty room. The curtains were still apart and the outside light poured in. He hastily drew the curtains and flopped on the bed contemplating. What if Jan had come out of Nora's room just as he had been coming out of Liz's? What would he say to Jan? But the question uppermost in his mind was "How can I exist without Liz and what she does to me?" He undressed, again, and got into bed to await Jan's return.

Liz purred with satisfaction. No need to pursue the others now, she had Steve and she could keep him for as long as she wanted. She had no pity for Jan as the pathetic creature was no match for her and did not possess the powers it had taken years to cultivate. She felt very safe. Steve wanted her now, but she had known all along he would, because that was how she worked.

This had been quite a devious little journey. Working on Jan to cause the little hiccups in their so called happy marriage, Nora taking poorly at her stall to get Jan out of the way to let her get started on Steve, and tonight. Bert didn't take much effort, and he would be fit again before long. Nora dear soul had to accompany her husband, and Jan always the caring little elf had to look after her. Oh the power of thought!

Meeting Martin had been an added bonus. Funny how things had a habit of working out for you, by fate laying little opportunities at your feet.

She turned her mind to Steve. "Not bad," she breathed "not bad for now."

The night porter watched the taxi stop outside the main entrance of the hotel. He recognised Nora and Jan at once and unlocked the door to welcome them in.

"Is your husband going to be all right madam?"

Before he could reccive an answer, Giles breezed in with Barbie on his arm.

"So sorry we're late old boy, what ho, you girls been on the town too? Must say it doesn't agree with you." and without waiting for a reply swept his companion to the lift. "Got my key" he called over his shoulder to the porter who stood openmouthed. The man turned back to Nora to apologise, but the two were already finding a seat on one of the comfy sofas.

"Let them get out of the way, I can't talk to them." Nora had barely the strength to speak.

"They've gone now, are you all right to go up?"

Nora nodded and as Jan dismissed the porter with a little wave of her hand, they slowly headed for Nora's room.

Bert had suffered a mild heart attack, and would stay in hospital for a while. Arrangements had to be made to collect the car and stock as Nora could not drive. She would contact their son in the morning and see if he could come down by train and take care of things. She would stay on, perhaps at a bed and breakfast nearer the hospital until her husband was able to travel home.

"Just take each step as it comes." Steve had put on his dressing gown, unlocked the room and he and Jan were just waiting until Nora settled.

"Yes. Thank you, I don't know what I'd have done."

"Try and get some sleep," Jan tried to coax her, but did not hold out too much hope for it.

The Masters walked slowly back to their room hand in hand. Jan needed the close contact after supporting Nora. She felt quite drained. As soon as the door closed behind them, and they could enjoy their own privacy, Jan's arms went round her husband's neck and he responded with a burning guilt as he felt the familiar form of her pressed against him.

He still loved her so much, and could not understand how he could want anyone else. For the world he did not want to hurt Jan, she did not deserve it. What had she done? Nothing, except love him. At that point he made a decision. He had got to get Liz out of his system. Maybe easier said than done. Unfortunately, she held the trump card. She could always tell Jan, although it was her word against his, but he was only too well aware of her power over people.

"Angel." he whispered inches from her hair.

"Mmm."

"Why don't we have a holiday? It's nearly June and things will be fairly quiet soon. As soon as school breaks up let us jet off somewhere." "That should do it" he thought, "I won't see Liz, she won't know where I am, I can really get her out of my system. I have to."

"Oh Steve, could we. After every thing that has happened I think we deserve it." Jan although fatigued was elated at the prospect.

"We certainly do. It's late, let's get some sleep, we are both shattered." and they both undressed and fell into bed.

Steve lay with his back to Jan, determined in his mind to get Liz out of their lives and get back to normal. But it was the woman down the hall who was in his thoughts as he finally dropped off to sleep.

Chapter 14

August was hot. The fair circuit had been reasonably quiet as most people chose to be on outdoor pursuits, rather than indoor. Bert and Nora had returned home on the firm instruction that Bert was to take it very easy. That put them out of the running for a while and although they both missed the regulars, they were secretly glad of the enforced rest. Nora had sent a lovely card to Jan thanking her for the kindness she had shown when Bert was taken ill. Giles was doing his own thing, whatever it was, nobody cared, and little knowing what a lucky escape he had had. The Masters had been to Portugal for a week, thoroughly relaxed being absolutely idle, and Steve began to feel easier in his mind. The lads from 'We Are Stamps' kept the shops open between them, and took it in turns to have a holiday. Nobody had seen Liz.

Jan and Steve were stretched out on the patio on their loungers, when the 'phone rang.

"I'll go," Steve was already on his feet.

"Hello, Steve Masters speaking."

"Hello Steve, it's Tony"

After the initial pleasantries which Tony kept to the minimum he said "I'm standing at an antique and collectors' fair at Bournemouth, some exhibition centre, weekend after next. I'm not running it you understand, just standing."

"Sounds good." Steve waited for the punchline.

"I wondered if you would be interested in coming?"

"Let me call Jan." "Jan" he bellowed. As she joined him he asked "Just us Tony?"

"Only me from our firm, the others aren't bothered, but I made some good leads when we were there last and I can follow them up. Nora and Bert of course can't come, and Giles is somewhere in the Canaries. That just leaves Liz."

"You mean she isn't coming?" Steve tried to keep his voice even.

"No, sorry, didn't I make myself clear. She will be there."

"Just a second Tony." Steve hastily explained to Jan who said "Why not, let's go. Get the details."

Liz had slipped way back in Jan's mind. With not seeing her, life had become peaceful again, the threat had disappeared, so, standing near her at a fair would not bother her.

"Thanks very much Tony, we'll see you there then." Steve replaced the receiver and said "Tony will book it for us with the organiser but we have to make a hotel reservation. We go first thing on the Saturday morning, stand for two days and come home Sunday night. Bit hectic."

"That's O.K. you have no school and I will let the agency know I'm not available for the Monday."

Steve said casually, "There's just Tony, us and Liz.

"Fine, it will be a change to do an antique fair. Could have a look round if we are not too busy."

Steve felt some relief that Jan was looking forward to it, but his stomach churned when he admitted to himself just how much he was too. The past weeks had been idyllic, and he had made up his mind that Liz did not feature in his life, on a personal basis, anymore. He could not help wondering just how he would feel when he saw her again. He was already excited at the prospect and knew that, should an opportunity arise, he would not be as brave as he was trying to make out he was. To resist her would take every ounce of self control he could muster, but he was only too well aware of the speed at which her will took over. In her hotel room it had only taken minutes, or was it seconds for him to be lying in her embrace. Time seemed to evaporate with her as though she had control over it.

"Penny for them," Jan broke into his thoughts as she made a long cold drink.

"Oh yes, should we get some more stock?" Steve's mind was racing.

"Should be all right. Different lot of people I expect, not being a stamp fair."

"Yes, you're probably right, most of them won't have seen what we have already" and the two slowly strolled back to enjoy the sun.

Liz was vibrant with expectation. She had obtained her objective with Steve by letting him sample the pleasures in store for him, for she knew he could not resist her, given the opportunity. He was hers to play with for a while, but for this woman the excitement was not in the capture, it was in the chase. Therefore she was already lining up the next quarry. But, and there was a big 'but'. For the first time in her unsavoury life she felt different. At this stage of the game she would have been ready to cast aside her current achievement, and start hunting. The difference was Steve. For the first time Liz actually felt love. She could not remember when she had ever experienced this emotion, and had spent most of her time searching for that special something. Her carefully developed powers provided her with a strange hold over people, but that did not make any of them attracted to her, only to lust after her. A strange pang hit her stomach as she anticipated seeing him again.

"Maybe I need to find out just how much I need him and how far he is prepared to go to keep me." and she picked up a magazine, flicked carefully through the pages, until she found an article on cookery.

"Splendid." She cut out a picture of a well roasted chicken and sat with it in her hands, deeply meditating.

Tony stood back to cast a discerning eye over his handiwork.

"Let's hope this display stands up to Brian's heavy handedness. He did not mean it unkindly, but found the man to be very irritating at times. Well, most of the time, in fact. Mr. "ever efficient" Jennings checked his wants list to make sure he had everything he had been asked for by customers in the area of the fair. Having done his homework, he had already contacted most of them, and so had lined up quite a few sales.

"It will be nice to see Steve and Jan again," he thought to himself. After the affair with Martin, he and Steve seemed to have developed camaraderie, and after being in Brian's company, these two were like a breath of fresh air.

"I wonder what Liz meant by her last remark." She had 'phoned him a few times, always about something trivial, but when he had felt the urge to invite her to Bournemouth, she had replied "If you are going to be there, how could I not?"

"Not like her to come on to me" Tony was not sure if he liked the feeling. "Other men yes, but - - well perhaps she has anyone" and he dismissed the thought as being irrelevant.

Chapter 15

"Oh not today of all days." Jan's head was half way down the toilet.

"I wonder what made you sick, it must have been something you've eaten." Steve looked up as she joined him downstairs.

It was the Friday evening before the fair and Jan felt and looked ghastly.

"We've had the same food," she did not really want to dwell on the subject at the moment, but was curious all the same.

"Wait a minute, that place where I was working today, we all sent out for a sandwich."

"What did you have?"

"Chicken salad, but so did Fiona, no wait a minute, she changed her mind, she had ham." Jan was striving to remember if anyone else had eaten the same.

"What sort of place was it?" Steve had already formed the idea in his mind that it would be a little shop, not to keen on hygiene.

"A pub, the food is very good."

"Will you be O.K. for tomorrow?" The thought suddenly hit Steve, that if Jan would not be well enough, he would not see Liz.

"I think so. I'll have a good night's sleep, but I think I'll stick to plain food over the week end." Then she added "I'm sorry."

He smiled. "What have you got to be sorry about? Not your fault."

"I know, but we have been looking forward to this trip." She kissed him gently and with a parting smile went up to bed.

He sat alone. The thoughts would not stop pouring into his head. Not unpleasant, but expectant, exciting. Within hours he would see Liz. He hoped Jan would be well enough, for two reasons, and one was nothing to do with her state of health.

With relief Steve headed the car southwards. Jan although still feeling a bit queasy, had improved enough to travel. She nibbled cream crackers in an effort to keep her tummy settled, and after a fairly pleasant journey, she felt able to cope with the day.

The fair organiser had decided to put all the stamp dealers together with a couple of coin dealers in a small side room to make it easier for the specialised collectors. Tony weighed up the position, and requested that a sign be put up to show people where they were. It was agreed to put a "Stamp and Coin Dealers" sign, with an arrow just outside the room. Satisfied with this they all started to set up. There was no point in going all that way if customers could not find you.

Liz was placed between the Masters and Tony.

"Rather convenient," she pondered, "I can kill two birds." She looked towards Tony but apart from the odd glance he was intent on placing everything just where he wanted.

"She's seems to be leaving us alone." Steve had noticed the direction of Liz's attention, and felt a pang of jealousy.

Jan followed his gaze. "Thank goodness." Then nudged her husband's arm.

"She's history."

He hoped not. Steve felt the urge returning to taste the wine. He had only sipped, now he wanted to drink. To get drunk on it.

It did not suit Ms.Niebur to not be in control. It had never happened before, and she did not relish the idea of it happening now. Yet it was, because she could not, no, she dare not look towards that man without betraying her feelings. It was for this reason, she concentrated her intentions towards Tony, but without the same verve she had used on previous prey. He would do as a cover, she decided, but as soon as she could, she would have to let Steve know the reason for her apparent change of direction. This was also not typical of her nature, and she was only too well aware of it.

Tony was feeling decidedly uncomfortable. He did not have a steady girlfriend, not that he didn't like the young ladies, but it would take a very special one to put up with his fastidious habits. He considered there was plenty of time, and he was a very busy man, so it did not present a problem. Until now. Liz was standing very close to him as they looked at a penny red trying to decipher the plate number. He tried to move sideways, but found his escape blocked by the chair he had placed to hold his briefcase.

"Not a seventy seven." Liz was bent over peering through a magnifier.

"No such luck." Tony gave a short laugh. The possibility of finding such a stamp was unthinkable, and it was not even given a price in the stamp catalogues. If one was lucky enough to acquire one, the value would have to find its own level in auction.

As she straightened up, Tony felt the woman's presence enveloping him.

"I've got to stop this now." was his intention.

"I love red hair." her voice was barely audible.

"Do you? How nice for you." hoping his words were steady, he continued. "There is someone looking through your G.B.," and nodded towards her table.

"I'll be back." She slid from his stall to hers, without taking her eyes off him.

"I'm not going anywhere." he doubted that she would hear, but her smile proved she had. Liz Niebur's tail was beginning to wave again.

Saturday brought the shoppers who had "only come for a look round". Tony's preparation had reaped its rewards, which in turn provided a little stream past the others. Towards the end of the afternoon, and elderly gentleman approached Steve about selling his collection. After noting the address, he agreed with Tony and Liz to let them have first refusal of anything worthwhile, especially if there was a lot. He expected that Jan would go with him, but she was still feeling the effects of the sickness.

"It's been a long day and I think it's taken it out of me." she looked up at Steve.

"You do look a bit peaky."

"I'll probably just have some soup or something for dinner, then go to bed. I'll be much better tomorrow. You don't mind do you?" Her head was cocked to one side as she spoke.

"No of course not angel, I'd rather you got yourself right."

They all packed the good stock away, and covered the tables for the night. The manager of the centre had the wisdom to arrange for the room to be locked as soon as the dealers had left, but it would be unlocked as soon as the first one arrived in the morning. It was therefore up to the individual to protect their own interests.

Chapter 16

All three dealers were staying at different hotels. It was not the same as being on their own circuit, when they travelled together, this time it was more of an individual venture. Steve felt a twinge of disappointment as he realised he would not be seeing Liz until the next morning, and if Jan had felt more herself, she would have been delighted at the prospect. As it was, she just wanted to rid herself of this hollow sinking feeling.

After dinner the Masters had gone to their room.

"I won't be gone long" Steve checked his briefcase and wallet.

"Don't rush, you've got to find the place first."

"Yes" he looked at the note containing the address, and brief directions of how to get there.

"If I'm asleep, could you try not wake me up? I want to be all right for tomorrow."

"Of course, angel. You rest now." and he gave her a gentle kiss, then left.

The wonderful collection as described by the vendor was not all it had been made out to be. There were a couple of items which could be sold quickly to regain most of the cost, but the rest would take ages to offload. Many stamps were badly mounted, some even torn. Steve did not really want it so as kindly as he could, he tried to explain to the disappointed man that condition was very important when it came to value, and he could not offer him all that much. He stated a price and received the reaction he expected.

"It's nice of you to come and look at it, but I think I'll hang on to it just now, and have a think about it."

"Good job I don't charge for valuation," Steve felt a little deflated, "because that's about all he wanted."

"Hello handsome." Steve jumped as he unlocked his car.

"Liz! I didn't recognise you. How long have you been here?"

"Oh, just about as long as you. Any good?"

"What, oh the stamps. No. Usual load of crap"

It suddenly occurred to Steve why it was he had not recognised her. She was not dressed in black. Instead she wore a vivid orange silk trouser suit, with a matching narrow band holding her black locks behind her ears. Her make up was flattering, and she smelled delectable.

"If you are not in too much of a hurry, could we talk?" The invitation was unexpected, but nevertheless irresistible.

"Sure, but where?"

"Follow me." she was in her car in no time, and Steve had to move fast to keep up with her.

After a few minutes they had left the town, and were in open country. Steve followed as Liz swung off the road and parked in a small wooded area. He got out, locked his car and went over to join her.

"How did you know where to find me?" the thought had puzzled him throughout the journey.

"I have been standing next to you all day my dear, I could hardly miss where or when."

"I suppose not."

"I have missed you Steve." This was the last thing he expected to hear.

"I wouldn't have thought so." He couldn't help thinking of her attention to Tony.

"No, well I haven't exactly made a play for you today."

"You go in for understatements for a hobby?" he was smiling at her.

"Steve." Her voice almost trembled.

"Liz, come here." He need not have invited her as she was already in his arms, exchanging kisses fuelled by the burning fire they had both locked away for too long. It was inevitable that they would make love that night.

As they lay there on the soft grass under the trees in this haven of happiness, both wished that time would freeze and they could stay in this paradise for ever.

"How did you find this place, it's so secluded?" Steve wondered if she had been here before.

"I came down yesterday and had a nose around, in the hopes that we could somehow get together."

"So you have been here since then?"

"I certainly did not travel back."

"Liz, I thought I could live without you, but I know I can't. What are we going to do.?"

"Nothing."

"What do you mean nothing?" Steve was somewhat taken aback.

"Steve, you have a lot to learn. You cannot stop loving me, right?"

"That's right, that's what I'm trying to tell you."

"Well Steve, for once in my life, I feel the same."

He leaned over to kiss her, but she held him away for a moment.

"If someone feels an emotion strongly enough, then no one can do anything about it. If we share love, then it doesn't matter where we are or who we are with, the feeling will be the same."

"But how will I see you?" this was all a bit new to Steve.

"It will happen. Be patient."

"It still feels unreal."

Her voice was very deliberate as she slowly said "We will not be parted now." There was an uncanny ring to those words which kept repeating in Steve's ears as he drove back to the hotel.

Jan was, as he hoped, fast asleep when he gingerly crept into their room. This time he felt no guilt. He quickly got ready for bed and eased himself between the sheets so as not to waken her. The last thought through his mind as he dropped off to sleep was "We will not be parted now."

"I cannot believe how much better I feel." Jan sat eating a good breakfast, her colour returned. "It's as though a weight has been lifted from my body." she bubbled.

Steve looked at her. What was he going to do? Nothing. That is what Liz had almost ordered him. Nothing for now at least.

"Good. I'm glad you're feeling better"

"Did you get that collection you went to see?"

"No, no, it was not what we need." Steve was having to make polite conversation but had the feeling he was not being very good at it. He continued "We had better not be too late getting to the centre, we want to be there when they unlock the room." Then thought to himself "How do I face Liz? What do I say?"

They finished breakfast, cleared up their bedroom and checked out of the hotel. They were first at the venue, and had to wait for the manager to unlock the room for them.

"We can keep an eye on the others' stuff until they get here, although it is covered." Steve went to their table.

"There's often some impatient soul that tries to look underneath anyway." Jan said joining him.

"Good morning folks." Tony was almost on their heels. "Feeling better Jan? Must say you look it."

"Yes, I feel great this morning, thank you Tony."

The coin dealers arrived and with the usual chat about customers, stock, and the general contents of the Sunday papers the time crept on to the opening of the day's trading.

"Anyone seen Liz?" Steve was glad Tony had asked the question as it had been burning on his mind since they arrived.

"She's probably overslept." Jan voiced aloud and thought "Who with this time?"

The fair organiser appeared at the door and pointed towards Steve. He stood back and made way for a tall impressive looking man who headed straight for Steve and Jan.

"A customer I hope." Jan got her feet.

"Mr. Masters? Mr. Stephen Masters.?"

"That's me." Steve wondered if he had been sent by another dealer.

"Detective Inspector James. May I have a word with you please? Outside would be best."

Steve turned to Jan who said "What's it about ?"

"If you wouldn't mind sir?" The chief inspector was not going to give any indication of why he wanted Steve.

"Right, let's see what this is all about." Bewildered, Jan watched as her husband was escorted from the room.

Chapter 17

Liz Niebur was dead.

"Perhaps you had better sit down sir." Chief Inspector James ushered Steve to a chair in the small office provided by the centre for his enquiries.

"How? What happened? When was this?" he had so many questions, but above all "Why did you tell me?"

The officer ignored this barrage and asked in return "Where were you last night sir?"

"Why are you asking me that?"

"Just answer the question, if you wouldn't mind sir?"

"I went out to view a stamp collection somebody wanted to sell it, only I didn't buy it." Steve did not want to go into the details of his meeting, although it was beginning to look as though it would be dragged out of him.

"Then what happened?"

"I -er- happened to bump into Liz, look officer, does my wife really have to find out, she might not quite understand."

"I bet she won't. Go on please sir."

"Well we talked for a while, and then I went back to the hotel."

"What time would that be sir?"

"About half past ten, I think, my wife was asleep, but the owner might remember, I spoke to her."

"Good, we'll check that out. So you have a witness as to your whereabouts at half past ten, approximately."

"Yes, why is that so important, and can you tell me what has happened?"

"Miss Niebur was found early this morning by someone walking his dog on the sand. It appears she fell down the cliff path, or was helped. We will know more after we have the examination results. In her bag we found the name of the hotel where she was staying, and on visiting her room, we found a booking confirmation of this fair, and also a picture of you at the side of her bed. Your name was on the back."

"Where in heavens name did she get that?" Steve was trying to piece it all together.

"You did not know she had it sir?"

Steve had to think quickly. With Liz gone, Jan need never know anything that was going to hurt her. Not now.

"No. Look Chief Inspector, this woman has given us a bit of a hard time, chasing me, and I was not interested, and my wife has had enough of it." He hoped it sounded plausible, when all the time he wanted to cry out for his beloved Liz. He needed to grieve.

"I think that will be all for now, thank you sir, oh by the way, apart from your wife, what other dealers would have known the deceased?"

"Only Tony Jennings, as far as I am aware."

"Well I will have a word with him next, would you ask him to come in please?" the officer was giving an order and although Steve could not see that his colleague could be of any help, he agreed.

"We'll keep an eye on your stall Tony," Jan was anxious to find out what was going on.

Steve broke the news to his wife, and although it came as a shock, she could only feel a tremendous relief. No sorrow.

"Why do they want Tony?"

Steve shrugged, "They want to speak to anyone who knew her. It sounds awful in the past tense, so final."

The feelings experienced by the couple could not have been more opposite as they tried to concentrate on the day.

Tony appeared with Ch.Insp. James and a detective constable who had just arrived. The latter busied himself packing up the stock on Liz's stall, assisted by Jan who had more idea of how to transport this kind of merchandise. It was all going to be taken to the local police station for safe keeping, along with her car, until a relative could be traced.

As Steve was on his own at his stall, the Chief Inspector took the chance of saying quietly "The time of your arrival at the hotel has been verified, and as it seems you were not the last person to see the lady alive, you are free to go. There will of course be a post mortem, and an inquest, and if you would give your address and 'phone number to my officer, I would be most grateful. Just for the record, you understand. We need not bother your wife."

"Thank you very much, I appreciate that." the relief on Steve's face was very obvious.

As soon as the police had left, Steve turned to Jan and said "I must go and have a word with Tony, he looks quite shaken. You'll be O.K. won't you?"

Jan almost hissed "Go on then, but I wonder why he is so upset, do you reckon he and she were, well you know?"

"I doubt it," his stomach churned at the thought of it. "Be back in a minute."

Steve and Tony sat down behind the stall so that their voices did not carry to the other dealers in the room, especially Jan.

It appeared that Tony had met Liz purely by chance after she had left Steve. All of the hotels being used by the three parties were quite near to the cliff top. Liz had parked her car, and being thoroughly elated by the evening's events, decided to take a stroll and fill her lungs with the sea air. It was Tony's practice to take a constitutional last thing at night, and first thing in the morning.

The two had exchanged pleasantries at the top of the winding cliff path, when Liz had hinted to Tony that she had at last found happiness, but that all would be revealed very soon.

"What do you suppose she meant by that?" Tony enquired.

Steve was somewhat relieved that his friend had not guessed the truth. "I've no idea, but go on." He did not want too many searching questions.

"Well she was on a sort of high, and she said she wanted to run barefoot on the beach, so she turned and ran off down the path."

"And that was the last you saw of her?" Steve wanted every detail of her movements.

"Yes, I turned to go back to the hotel and nearly collided with a courting couple."

"What time was all this." Steve still wanted assurance that Tony had seen her after he did.

"I got back to the hotel at eleven, and it's only a couple of minutes walk."

"So, what is happening now?" Steve, having experienced his own examination, could not envisage the Chief Inspector leaving it at that.

"They have verified when I got back, but they are going to try and find witnesses who saw me leave her, they especially want to trace the courting couple."

"Have you got to stay here?"

"No. They think I am a reliable sort, and they have all my business details so I can go for now. It is likely the inquest will be opened and adjourned until they can find the witnesses."

"I'm sure they will." Steve tried to sound reassuring, but his heart was empty.

Tony's name was cleared. There had been no evidence of a struggle, and the marks on Liz's body indicated she had slipped on the path, and plunged to her death. The couple had come forward, feeling it was their claim to fame, and explicitly described Tony nearly knocking them off their feet as he waved to this woman in the orange suit. A verdict of accidental death was recorded, and life struggled to return to normal.

It was early September, and life in the Masters' house seemed normal enough. Jan still felt as though a weight had been lifted, and did not notice her husband's inner turmoil. He had not had the opportunity to pour out his grief, and it was still locked away inside him.

This was obscuring one very important fact. He did not love Liz, he thought he did, and what had been merely lust, deceived him into believing it was love. Had the affair only continued a little longer, he would have come to his senses, regardless of what Liz had felt, and he would have realised how his stupidity had jeopardised his relationship with Jan. The thought therefore had not yet crossed his sad mind of how Liz would cope with rejection. Nobody would ever know what the outcome would have been. Nobody needed to.

They were returning from the usual weekly shopping trip.

"I wonder who that belongs to. Don't remember seeing it before." Jan was gathering up the carrier bags and making her way to the house.

Steve followed with the remaining groceries, and his eyes caught the object of her statement. There sitting on the wall was a black cat, gently waving it's tail. As the heartbroken man drew level with it, he stood transfixed as the green eyes narrowed to mere slits, and held his gaze. The transmitted thought hit his mind like a bullet as he realised he would never be alone again.

"We will not be parted now."

===

Printed in Great Britain
by Amazon